SON of MAN

a novel by
Andrew Klavan

THE PERMANENT PRESS
SAG HARBOR, NEW YORK 11963

Library of Congress Number: 87-62808
International Standard Book Number: 0-932966-86-1

Manufactured in the United States of America

THE PERMANENT PRESS
Noyac Road
Sag Harbor, NY 11963

The poem of the transfiguration was originally published under the title "Son of Man" by *Amelia* magazine, as winner of their 1985 Charles William Duke Longpoem Award.

This book is for Faith

Winsome M. Fraser-Holness
12/31/94

PART I: BAPTISM

1. This is the beginning of The Collector's Journal, containing the first of the poems in the Jesus cycle.

Jesus was born in Nazareth, a town in Galilee of about fifteen thousand souls. He was the second son of Mary, a carpenter's wife. His older brother was named Joses, and he had later a younger brother named James. He also had two sisters whose names and ages I could not discover.

Jesus' father was Joseph, an amiable and hard-working builder of houses and farming tools. He is remembered fondly among his people for his clever and outgoing personality and for his skill at his craft.

Those who remember the birth of Jesus say it was attended to in the usual manner of the Jews. When her time arrived, Mary was taken indoors by the midwives. She was given a mixture of herbs and wine to drink against the pain of labor, and handed, too, a dead animal—possibly a scorpion—to clutch for good luck. When the newborn arrived, he was lifted from the afterbirth by the attending women, bathed in water, then rubbed in salt. Next, the women wrapped him tightly in swaddling clothes and laid him in a trough they used as a cradle.

After eight days, the boy was taken to the local synagogue to be circumcised, according to the custom of his people. Mary had to stay behind: for seven days after the birth, she was considered unclean, and for thirty-three days more, she had still to remain sequestered. When the time of the circumcision arrived, the infant Jesus was taken from his mother's arms by his godmother. She carried him across the square into the synagogue.

As she stepped from the daylight into the darkness of the stone building, the congregation within rose from the benches and sang, "Blessed be he who comes in the name of the Lord!" At the candlelit altar at the front of the room, the town barber, acting in his religious capacity as *mohel,* proclaimed, "I am about to fulfill the precept of my creator."

The baby was brought forward, set upon a bench and held there by his godfather. A brief blessing was said and a drop of wine placed in the baby's mouth. Then, the child was exposed. The *mohel* grasped Jesus' penis and pulled the foreskin over the head before slicing the foreskin away with a bone knife. Then, the *mohel* performed the operation called *periah* in which the membrane around the baby's glans was also cut away. This extremely painful and somewhat complicated procedure makes it more difficult to disguise the traces of circumcision in later life—as many Jews try to do in the hopes of mixing in with their gentile neighbors.

Finally, the *mohel* put Jesus' penis in his mouth and sucked the blood from the wound in order to cleanse it. Then he said: "God hath impressed His seal on our flesh that all who see us may know and recognize that we are the seed which the Lord hath blessed."

When the prayers were over, the infant was handed to Joseph, who was asked the name of the child. He replied: "The child's name is Jesus: God is our savior."

At the age of thirteen, Jesus became *bar mitzvah*: son of the law, or he who may be punished for his transgressions. In that year, Joseph and Mary took their family to Jerusalem for the Passover. This is the Jews' spring festival, in which they celebrate their freedom from slavery in Egypt: that freedom won, they say, by virtue of a plague sent by their Lord to claim the sons of the Egyptians.

The procession to Jerusalem took three days. On the first, the families of Nazareth gathered at the town's well with their wagons and mules. The men took their staffs in their hands and the women their babies. The command was given and the caravan set off. They traveled on a road between grassy plains with the misty hills of Galilee on the horizon beyond them. At every town, new pilgrims joined them, until the road was glutted with men, women and children; camels, mules, oxen and wagons—all surrounded by a haze of dust, and a babble of talk and song.

Climbing over the hills into the valley of the Jordan River, they stayed the first night among the cities of the Decapolis, which are modern, many of them, their buildings and temples and colonnades made of gleaming marble and stone. On the morning of the second day, they moved on beside the river, into the wilderness of Judea. They camped by the oasis of Jericho, where the rich make their summer homes.

Finally, on the third day, the numberless throng saw the wasteland end. Under the watchtowers from which Roman guards observed them, they entered the gardens and fields of the city suburbs. Like a great snake, they wound around the base of the Mount of Olives and, at last, each in his turn looked upon Jerusalem.

Joseph made camp with his fellow townspeople. Then, he and the men of Nazareth—including Jesus now—ventured into the city to buy a lamb for the holiday sacrifice: a ritual which propitiates their God for the sons of Israel who were all miraculously spared by the Egyptian plague.

The Great Temple of Jerusalem sat on the city's highest hill. It consisted of a huge open courtyard with the temple itself at the center. Within the courtyard were the brightly colored booths of merchants: money exchangers who served the foreigners so that they could purchase animals for sacrifice, and those who sold the animals themselves. Above the court, and connected to its wall by a bridge, was the Antonia fortress. From there, Roman soldiers looked down upon the ceremonies and policed the crowd, for it was on these religious occasions that violence and uprisings were most likely to occur.

When the Nazarenes had pushed into the courtyard and bought their lambs, they joined two lines. At the end of each stood a priest, ready to perform the sacrifice. Young Jesus' description of this sacrifice forms the first poem in the collection:

No one spoke the name of the Lord,
the God of Abraham.
No, nobody spoke the name of the Lord
in the place where he calls the lamb.

There a man with a nose like a talon,
and a thirst for his gold by the gallon,
and the heat of his thirst in his eyes,
sold us the sacrifice.

And the lamb was white.
And I held him tight.

The priest's robes shone with cloth-of-gold
and jewels along its seam
and his face, as sad as a saint of old,
seemed alight with the golden gleam.

When the shofar *moaned like a roiling beast,*
we formed a procession behind the priest,
till he reached the altar, turned and stood.
And it was stained with blood.

The horn of the ram
called the trembling lamb.

'Oh, praise the Lord,' the priest then sang.
And now the shofar *roared.*
'Praise his name forever,' the priest's voice rang.
But none spoke the name of the Lord.

'Not us, not us but just His name,' the priest then cried.
'Not us, not us but just His name be glorified.'
But no one around the blood-stained board
spoke the name of the Lord.

Not the priest most high.
Nor I.

He took my lamb, pulled back its head,
held it above a bowl.
When he raised his dagger his face glowed red,
as his robe gleamed with cloth-of-gold.

Son of Man

The lamb strained as a gash beneath his fleece
swallowed the dagger. Then the straining ceased.
He sagged. The blood, as it pattered down,
was now the only sound.

God of Abraham,
my gift of a lamb.

I looked away while it was dressed—
while Father took two pegs,
and ran one up from its rump to its breast,
and one cross its two front legs.

But the paschal feast was as mine alone.
I ate and grew heavy. The full moon shone,
till dawn was big with the waiting day;
my soul with the need to pray:

To bring forth the lamb;
and the name: I AM.

When the festival was over, Joseph and Mary and the other Nazarenes made preparations to go. But as the caravan was being packed, Joses approached his parents and told them that Jesus was nowhere to be found.

A frantic search for the young man began. It was feared he was lost or that he had come to harm among the many disreputable people in the city. At last, however, Mary suggested they look for him in the temple, because she knew he had been deeply moved by the ceremonies there and had wanted to see the place again.

They found Jesus in the temple courtyard, sitting among a group of scribes, men who were considered expert in Jewish law. The conversation had drawn a small crowd, because the young boy spoke in a rebellious yet eloquent manner that had left the older men discomfited. The people were amused and they urged Jesus on.

"Do you really think the Lord is in your rules and regulations?" Jesus said. "You're breaking the chalice to sell the jewels. You're like merchants holding the shards of scripture to the light, twirling them in your fingers and looking for a freak strain to make your fortune with—or pausing, suddenly, entranced by your own reflection there. I feel . . . I've seen . . . seen . . ."

But here Jesus became so impassioned he could no longer speak. And yet he might have gone on, had not Joseph and Mary stepped forward and intervened. They were angry with their son for having wandered off and frightened them—and also for insulting men of authority.

Joseph shouted at him: "What is the meaning of this? Why did you wander off when we were ready to go? Didn't you realize how worried we'd be? We looked all over for you."

Jesus was embarrassed to be publicly treated as a child. He answered fiercely: "Leave me alone. I am going about *my* Father's business," referring to the god of his people.

At this, Joseph lost his temper and would have struck the boy. But Mary stepped between them, saying: "Now that we have found him, let's just go home."

Joseph turned away. He muttered: "Spoil him then. He's yours."

Now, Mary spoke to the boy roughly, ordering him to follow. But that was all. She had been married to the prosperous carpenter out of a house of poor but scholarly men: She had respect for her son's learning, and she kept his sayings in her heart.

The family returned to the caravan in silent anger, and so journeyed home to Nazareth.

2. This now is the beginning of The Book of Judas.

In the days when Rome first ruled over Palestine, Caesar Augustus sent Coponius to govern the Jews and to have full power over them. And Judas at this time was six years old, the only child of Benjamin and Judith of Sepphoris, which is the city that sits on the mountain top.

And Coponius decreed that there should be a census taken of the people that they might pay taxes to Caesar and come under his administration.

Now there was at that time in Sepphoris, a man called the Galilean.

And he went to the synagogue and called together many of the men of the town and addressed them, saying:

"My heart cries, and the heart of my God cries:
A king is raised above us
and the face of eagles graven in the place of the Lord."

And he called on the people to pay tribute to no one but the Lord, and to rise up in revolt against the census. And the people joined with him. And Benjamin, the father of Judas, and Abraham of Magdala, who was his friend, were also among them and joined with him.

And the people ran to the palace in the city where the guards of Antipas were. And the Galilean gave orders, crying: "Let us storm the walls, for this is the day of our liberation."

Then the Galilean led the charge with a multitude at his back. And they were shouting in anger and bearing aloft firebrands.

And the guards defended the portal with swords and many of the Galilean's men were killed so that the bodies piled up in the courtyard and the survivors had to scale the hillocks of the dead to strike at their enemies. And the Galilean cried out:

"This is the way to the oppressor
which he has paved with the lives of my companions.
Now he has made me such a road
that there is no returning on it."

In the last hour of the evening, the guards were overcome. And the people streamed into the palace and broke open the caches of weapons there until every man was armed.

Then the Galilean gave orders that the city should be fortified. "For surely," he said, "The Romans will storm the hill."

It was at this time that Sulpicius Quirinius, the Roman governor of Syria, determined that he would invade Judea to put an end to the great rebellions that had arisen there. Whereupon, coming from the north into the land of Galilee, he found revolts in numerous places, and made haste first to Sepphoris to quell the uprising.

And when daylight came, the Galilean and his men saw the army from the battlements of the city, and it was as if the horizon had opened to pour forth soldiers and horsemen with the rays of the rising sun. And the people fell back from the fortifications in terror.

And Quirinius swept down upon the city and set it on fire,

so that the houses of the people became walls of flame and the streets were corridors of smoke between them. And in the midst of the smoke was the thunder of horses. And swords flashed out of the smoke, their blades bright with the firelight, so that the people of the city died in great numbers seeing only the murderous sword and never the hand that held it.

Benjamin, the father of Judas, and Abraham, fought side by side all through that day; and many Romans fell by their swords. But, at last, Abraham lost his friend in the smoke.

And when he saw that the battle was finished and the Romans victorious, Abraham joined the great crush of people running from the city. And he made away with them to the surrounding hills.

And Abraham went to the place where the people gathered in the caves of the hills, and there he watched the city burning all night long. And the Romans put many of the people to the sword and many were taken away as slaves. And the Romans set crosses outside the city and crucified many of the people such that those who escaped could see them dying by the dying light of the flames. And Abraham wept in his heart because he knew that Benjamin was among them.

And when Abraham had seen these things, the women came to him and told him that the son of Benjamin had survived. For they had found him sitting in tears beside the body of his mother and they had carried him away beneath their robes.

And Abraham saw Judas sitting among the women. And the child sat watching the destruction of the city, and he cried out in his heart:

"I have seen the centurion with the sight of my eyes:
his stallion rearing,

the plume of his helmet waving,
his sword forever rising against the sky.
I have seen his breastplate glittering in the sun
and his red cape fluttering in the wind of the fire.
He has ridden on, and I see his shadow
still before me in the empty air."

And Abraham went to Judas and lifted the boy in his arms and said: "You are my son now."

Now when the country had become more peaceful, Abraham removed Judas to his home in Magdala on Lake Gennesaret. And Naomi, Abraham's wife, welcomed Judas joyfully, for she was childless.

And Abraham showed Judas the life of a fisherman on Gennesaret. And the boy grew strong and bold in spirit.

And Abraham told Judas of Sepphoris and of how he and Benjamin had fought bravely together so that many Romans died at their hands. And Judas listened and Rome was always in his thoughts. And he asked passing travelers of the wonders they had seen at Rome, and for himself saw the roads and the buildings they had made in the country and the lawfulness their soldiers had brought to the land.

But one day, when Judas was a young man, he saw a contingent of centurious riding along the road to the outpost at Capernaum. And Judas' heart was filled with anger, and he said:

"Where is the nation like you, Rome,
that has conquered my people?

I must be mighty as you are to reclaim them,
and wear a Roman face in battle with you."

Then Judas swore himself to be a rebel. And he carried the knife of the assassin which is called sicarius, and was known as Judas Sicariot.

Now about this time, the Romans sent Pontius Pilate to be procurator of Judea, Samaria and Idumaea, and ordered him to make Roman rule heavy on the shoulders of the people. And Pilate was appointed by Sejanus, who hated the Jews; and Pilate knew that Sejanus envied him his birth and would bring him to ruin if he failed in his appointment.

So Pilate sent his armies into Jerusalem and hung their standards from Antonia palace so that the graven image of the eagle should be above the house of the Lord. And the people were made angry and came before Pilate in Caesarea in great numbers, demanding the eagles be taken down.

Now when the people had cried out to him many days, Pilate ordered that they come to him in the stadium where he would issue his decree. And when they had come before him and made their request, Pilate lifted his finger and, at once, soldiers bearing naked swords entered at all the doorways. And the soldiers surrounded the people as if they would put them to death.

And the people bowed down before Pilate as one man, and bared their necks to him, so much as to say: Better we should die than that a graven image should hang above the temple.

And the procurator was amazed. And his lieutenant turned to him and said: "Pontius Pilate, meet the Jews."

And Pilate ordered that the eagles be removed.

Now when Judas heard of this, he traveled to Jerusalem for

the Passover, because he knew that Pilate would also be there and he hoped to make trouble against him.

And Pilate sent forth a proclamation, saying, "I will build an aqueduct for the city (as requested by Arras and others of your leaders) that will bring water from the Pools of Solomon that the water of the city may be pure and plentiful. And I will levy a special tax for this aqueduct upon the temple funds."

When the people were told that Pilate would despoil the sacred treasury of the temple, a great uproar arose among them. And the sacrifices ceased in the courtyard, and the people gathered together there to decide what they should do.

And Pilate sent agents to the courtyard who would speak for him that it might appear a fight had broken out among the people. And when the people had begun to argue, Pilate ordered his soldiers to keep the peace. And the soldiers charged the courtyard with swords and spears, and the blood of the people was mixed with the blood of the lambs.

Then Judas, who was in the city at that time, gathered some of his fellow Galileans around him. And he cried out to them in a loud voice, saying:

"Now, hear Judas speak.
Your fathers fought beside my father
and you, their children, played beside his child.
Here is Levi, who was Antony to my Pompey
among the quiet boats of Magdala,
and there is Saul—or Scipio—who held the Po
while I, as Hannibal, assaulted it.
But that was Galilee in childhood.
This is Jerusalem and war.

16

The Romans do to us what Romans would not bear.
Let us not endure it like the conquered Jews
but seek revenge."

And many greeted his speech with wild cheers and at once rushed back to Galilee in fear of their lives. But some remained, and when the days of the feast were over, Judas led them as a band to a pass on the road to Caesarea, for he knew the soldiers would return there for the spring.

And the rebels waited on a high rock above the pass. And when they heard the sound of the centurions' horses, they were afraid. But Judas said:

"A pulse will beat along this sword into my pulse,
and I am dead until a Roman life is mine."

And when plumes of dust rose up around the entrance to the pass, the rebels were afraid and trembled. But Judas said:

"We are the legacy of the brave
and will write their story
in the blood of conquerors."

And when the soldiers on horseback burst into the pass, Judas gave a bold yell and leapt among them, brandishing his sword. And all the rebels also gave bold yells and leapt, their swords upraised. And the Romans slaughtered them swiftly.

And Judas remembered the stories of Abraham and fought bravely, slashing with his sword to left and right. But he was also amazed, because he could see nothing but dust. And his ears were filled with the screams of the horses and the wails of his companions, and his mouth and nostrils were filled with dust. And the bridled teeth of the horses lunged at him suddenly out of the dust so that he fell to the ground. And the Roman swords flashed over him without warning out of the dust and then vanished so that he could not find his enemy. And Abraham's stories seemed a dream to him in the nightmare of dust and swords and screaming.

And then, suddenly, the dust was gone from around him. And Judas looked up and saw a mounted centurion above him, black against the sky with his sword raised, ready to slaughter him. And when Judas stopped running, he was in the surrounding hills with a few of his companions who had also survived. And the wounded were left behind to be crucified or taken slaves.

And when he was hidden in the hills, Judas remembered again the stories of Abraham. And he was sick with grief because he had led his companions to their destruction, and he himself had lived to run away.

3. Here, The Collector's Journal continues, including the second poem in the Jesus cycle.

In the fifteenth year of the reign of the emperor Tiberius, there appeared in the Jordan Valley a man by the name of John. He was a preacher of remarkable power; utterly fearless, because he recognized no authority but the God of his tribe. For this reason, too, the people loved him. His teachings seemed inspired to them, and they came to the shores of the river in great numbers to hear him speak. His aim was to induce in his followers an experience he called *metanoia,* which is to say: a complete and sudden transformation of the heart. This experience he signified by cleansing those who came to him in the waters of the river. He was therefore known as John the Baptist.

As his fame spread, he established, with his acolytes, a community in the Judaean wilderness. Here he lived with admirable austerity and discipline, eating only what he needed to survive, and claiming ownership of nothing but the pelt he wore upon his shoulders. Because of his appearance, the Romans laughed at him and said that he thought he was Hercules or Apollo. But among the people, there was speculation as to whether he might be the messiah: a leader who—as the Hebrew prophets claim—is destined to establish their God's dominion over the world.

Many miraculous stories grew up around this man, especially concerning his paternity, which was said to be royal or even divine. In truth, however, the Baptist seems to have been no more than the bastard child of a merchant's daughter. One day, when her father's caravan was headed north toward the Jordan crossing into Peraea, the unhappy woman decided to leave her infant son at a nearby monastery for the monks to raise. This she did, and the boy was taken in to grow up among the monks who call themselves Essenes and to be indoctrinated into the ways of their sect.

Now even among the Romans, the Essenes were regarded as holy men: chaste; poor; strictly observant of their religious vows. It was here John learned the ritual of baptism, the discipline of monastic farming life and many of the arcane notions of God which he later preached to the people. But as he grew older, he began to chafe at the severity of his upbringing, for he was a red-haired man with a heavy beard and a robust physique, such as are known to mark a quick temper and hot blood. When he came to manhood, he abandoned the monastery, rejecting the cloistered life he had been forced to live.

He traveled first to Caesarea where he found work as a dock laborer for the merchant ships. He lived wild among the Hellenes, and there are those to this day who claim to remember him as a man fast with his wits and his fists; a tavern singer with a fine voice; a lover of wine and a favorite among the prostitutes of the harbor.

Still, his appetites, so long neglected, were not yet satisfied. Daily, he watched the ships sail away to trade at distant ports-of-call, and he soon conceived a yearning to have the sea's reach of the world.

He became a sailor. He traveled the Mediterranean in merchant ships and for many years he lived out his wildest ideas of adventure. He soon became aware, however, that this way of life gave him no pleasure; in fact, if anything, his outlook was becoming darker and more brooding. He found it required greater and greater efforts to excite his sensations. He drank more heavily. He treated women cruelly. He took no man into his confidence. He was alone.

On his final voyage, his ship was set upon and boarded by pirates. The merchants managed to repel them, and even captured one: a yound boy abandoned in the crush of retreat. That night, John and his comrades celebrated their victory. They grew very drunk on wine, and soon, they were bragging and urging each other on to violence. At last, they descended as a mob on the boy, who sat chained on the deck. They tortured him all through the night: butchered him without killing him, and then killed him. And though John himself took no part in it, he looked on silently, his eyes bright, his blood hot.

He returned to Caesarea from that voyage a changed man. He removed his sailor's earrings for good and with them, it seemed, his gaiety and his daring. For a few weeks, he remained in the city, a gray figure, haunting the harbor, muttering to himself sometimes as if in argument with an invisible demon. His former companions could not cheer him nor could his former loves entice him. When they approached him, he said only, "Too much sorrow, too much sorrow," before drifting away. At last, one morning, he simply vanished: that is, Caesarea saw no more of him.

He wandered awhile through the cities of the Decapolis. He took up with a young widow in one town, but she soon died of fever. John moved on. Finally, he came to the neighborhood of his youth: the wasteland of Judaea. He stood on the banks of the Jordan, wondering whether to return to the monastery of the Essenes or go on alone. And when he had made up his mind, he lifted a sturdy branch that lay half in the water and half on land. Using this as a staff, he slowly plodded away into the barren country.

There, where the crags of brown and purple rocks seem to stretch on forever, and the wan sky looks the very color of indifference, and the fruitless earth is everywhere before the eyes like a reminder of mortality—there, like Jacob of whom the Hebrews tell, John wrestled with the angel.

His soul was feverish with grief. Even he did not know the cause of it. At one moment, his life appeared to him to be the judgment of holy wrath; at the next, it seemed merely capricious and miserable. He was beset by visions of the wasteland and his past. He cursed the mother who abandoned him and the monks who reared him. He clenched his fists at heaven and raged. He sat with his head between his knees and wept. Sometimes he fasted and sometimes he prayed, but both God and his own soul, like the earth around him, seemed barren to their horizons. He stood alone, crying out his mortality to a desert that could only echo it back again.

He was, at this time, a little older than thirty, although even he was unsure of his exact age.

Now, one day, John came out of the wilderness and down to the waters of the Jordan River. He had been away more than a month. He was malnourished and ill. His clothes were in tatters and alive with vermin. Large, painful boils had erupted on his skin. He undressed and waded into the water to wash himself.

When he was waist deep in the river, he stood still. The Jordan being wide at that point, the water was placid. He could see his face reflected on its surface. His red beard was filthy and overgrown, his hair wild, and his cheeks taut and craggy with anxiety. Through the image of his own features, in the water below, he could see the small fishes gathering to inspect his naked loins; and all around him were reflected the blue sky with its large, still clouds, the green trees and scrub that crowded the river banks and, in one concentrated, blinding ball of light, the sun, just arcing downward from its peak. Thirsty from his journey out of the desert, he bent down and dipped his cupped hands into the water—and, at once, his face, his loins, and the fish below, the sky and the trees above were shattered in ripples which dispersed the central radiance of the sun into a thousand sparks and flashes everywhere that erased even the river with their brilliance.

And his heart turned in that instant, that single second, from despair to elation. There was, suddenly, nothing before him but the coolness of the water and the sweetness of the light. The coolness of the water and the sweetness of the light—that was all. And John lifted up his face and sang a song of praise and thanksgiving. A blessing on the coolness of the water: the coolness of the water and the sweetness of the light. A benediction.

That is the story of John's *metanoia*. It was still some time before he became a preacher. But soon enough, he was wandering through the towns about proclaiming what he called the Good News, and crying out to the people: "Prepare in your heart the way of the Lord."

In time, he had many followers, and he established a permanent community near the town of Bethabara. It was modeled on that of the Essenes but free of many of its constraints. Some lived there, for instance, with their wives, and though John himself never married, he was not celibate, or so there is reason to believe.

With the community as his base, he went out frequently to the river to preach and perform baptisms. His fame spread far and wide throughout Palestine.

And so, in Nazareth, Jesus began to hear stories of him.

Jesus was thirty years old now. His father had died, and he and his brothers worked in the shop in his stead. Jesus hated this life. He found the work monotonous and his older brother's authority oppressive. Though he was of obscure ancestry, he had dreams of becoming a religious man—even a man of greatness like Hillel, who had led the Sanhedrin. When he heard that John was believed to be a prophet, like those in scripture, he resolved to go to him and join his community.

One night at dinner, he brought this matter before his family. At once, his mother was up in arms. "This is madness," she said to him. "To join with a man who angers the authorities! He'll bring trouble on his own head and on those around him. You will get yourself killed."

And Jesus answered: "Don't foist your fears on me, mother. I've been in this house too long."

"Get married, then, like your brothers," Mary said.

But Jesus said: "I will go to see the Baptist. How many times have you told me how your own father left his father's kilns and potter's wheels to study in Jerusalem."

"What did it ever bring him," cried his mother, "but the need to sell his daughters like cattle?"

And at this, she burst into tears and ran from the house.

24

Now Joses chimed in. "What kind of man are you who would abandon the support of your mother?" he said.

"I am the kind of man who cannot spend his life joining pieces of wood together," said Jesus.

Joses shouted: "That is an insult to your father."

"Or waste his thoughts deciding how to turn one penny into two and two into five and five into fifty when they are all worthless."

"Who is this John that you would give him authority over you?" Joses asked.

And Jesus answered: "Who are you?"

Joses was angry. "Who made this business what it is?" he said. "Who fed you and clothed you and kept a roof above you?"

Jesus glared at him and said quietly: "I will go to see the Baptist."

Through all this, Jesus' younger brother, James, looked on in silence. But the next morning, when he saw that Jesus would not come to work but stayed inside preparing for the journey to Bethabara, he went to him.

And Jesus said: "Are you also against me?"

"No," said James. "I wish you well. As Joses says, there are no prophets anymore. And as our mother says, you will probably get yourself killed. But as you say, this is no life for you. And I say: I wish you well."

So Jesus set off on his own for Bethabara, and his journey is the subject of the second poem in the collection:

Do not daydream so, my soul.
Fear not, and seek the way.
The child has had his little say:

Son of Man

the slave, who's master of the dark;
and here, where we have come of age,
his vengeance echoes and grows old
but never finds its mark
among the dead targets of his rage.

Only terror has wings;
God is god of the seen things.

Let the voice of the life I own be born,
and the voice of the prophet drown the voice
of a mother's fear and a father's scorn
and a brother's choice that is not my choice,
while the nightword
at moonset
once heard
forget.

Only terror has wings.
God is god of the seen things.

God is god of the seen things:
of the green leas
where the prey's eyes
through the laced trees
sweep the deep skies
till its sights freeze
where the hawk flies
on the high breeze.
Only terror has wings.

4. This is the beginning of The Tale of Mary Magdalene.

One morning, Mary is walking by the sea. And she thinks: "Look at them, ah, the boys are coming in, coming in off the water, half naked ain't they and the women waiting, the wives, all of them with their big hips and the skirts hung from them blowing in the breeze off the sea. I like the water when it's like this, first thing. Early in the morning with the blue reflection of the sky, and the white reflection of the clouds all shivering and mixed together on it. Even the colored kerchiefs of the wives above the yellow sand I like, and the sound of the women laughing sort of floating up lazy on the wind to me. Why do they laugh, the wives? And lean their heads together to whisper with their wry faces? Like they were making fun of the boys and bragging about their own to each other both at once? And the boys as they come in, look at them: holding up the fishes for the girls to see, and wrestling in the prows with each other to impress them. They're impressed, all right, too, for all their laughing. Trusting sows, really. The boys'll lay their fish in their baskets and it's the girls who haul the baskets away. Gut the catch and sell it and cook it and serve it while the boys, they come to me. They don't know. The wives don't know. I know. When it's all a stiff dingus and no talk of love, they wag their souls on the tip of their skin then, don't they? And they come to me."

She turns her back and walks away from the beach into town, and she thinks: "Still, it's the only time I can stomach

27

this place is when they're down there. It's kind of nice now. Dark and cooler on the winding cobble road before the sun comes up and bakes it, and the gray walls of the empty houses keeping you company on either side and not yet bright enough to blind you with the heat fairly breathing off of them and taking your own breath away, like they get later. And you can hear the little ones playing in the courtyards and they laugh so it sounds like bells out here. And their funny little songs. Reminds me of the way when I was little, I'd be collecting pebbles in a bucket in the backyard and it'd be such serious business. They sing that way, like it takes up all of them. And, anyway, no one to yell at you and call you names except the old ones and they're all gabbling at the well in the square. Market day today. Think I'll go to the square and tease some of the new figs out of one of the sellers. I've a hankering for figs. And anyway, who are those women to yell at me or keep me away? I saw Michael down there on the boat. Little woman waving to him all flushed and proud. And him half naked and brown with the white sail billowing and blowing out behind him. In the dark, he tells her, leans close to her ear with that long skinny stick he has poking at her thigh, and he tells her: I love you, you're precious to me, you're something to me, you're something, you're there. That's what she hauls and guts and cooks and serves him to hear. You're there, darling, feel yourself there where you weren't before. That's the lie he tells, the toll he pays to get at what she's got and her keeping it all shiny and new for him because a man likes to put his mark on everything and if it's been done before, he thinks it ain't worth doing. And she—she, she takes the toll and grateful for it because if it's him and it's just him, and there are babies to show, then she can pretend for a minute she's not a piece of

meat on the way out like the rest of us. She can close her eyes
and ride his cock up inside herself . . . pretend it's love. Only
loving herself really. Riding him into herself, seeding herself,
trying to grow a little out of herself. It's no wonder they come
to me."

She enters the town square, and she thinks: "All right, so
there they are. Fine. Fine. God damn it, look at them. And
when Michael comes to me, oh, when Michael comes to me
the talk is not so fine. He likes a little fuckme, fuckme chatter,
that's what makes him blast quick enough to make a profit off
him. Old bitches, staring at me. That's right. A little fuckme
fuckme shit shit shit on me, Michael, he likes to hear me say.
Yeah, the same to you, old bitch, don't look at me that way, I
know what makes all your daughters' husbands cum, and all
your sons, and your own husbands, too, if you want to know.
Which of them play at rape, and which of them like to paint
themselves like girls, and which brown hole me, and which of
them take a switch across their buns and spew, and which ones
nurse like babies, and which ones like to watch you shit while
all their pretending drip-drip-drips away in the first pearly
drop of scum that leaves them hard and moaning and who they
are. God damn it. God damn it, why did I come here I'm so
stupid sometimes. So sit there, old bitches, cunts, in your
shawls and manners. Takes them half a day to draw a little
water from the well gossiping this one takes a little wine, and
this one blasphemed on the Sabbath, if they only knew. And
market day, to see them hang above a pomegranate like a
vulture with their heads shaking unsure and their dried-up
claws hanging above their purses so you'd think they were
buying rubies for their crowns, wouldn't you? I don't even
know why I came here if it's going to be all that again. It's

because I like the colored awnings, that's why. The green and white stripes and the red and white stripes all fluttering over the fruits in rows of red, green, yellow, purple, ever so bright. Fuck it, though, if they're going to stare like that. I'm for the tavern. I need . . ."

She leaves the square, and enters a squalid district, and she thinks: ". . . some sleep for when their boys come cause they won't be calling for Ruth that's certain, or not half as much as they do for me, cause I've got the meat on me and they don't hang hesitating over my pomegranates. Ruth they'll only take from behind, it's the only soft part of her, and she can complain about it all she likes but if it weren't for her ass she'd be out of business. Oh, pop your eyes back in your head, Father, you can barely piss with it anymore. Anyway, she's getting on, Ruthie, twenty-five under the lies, and they tell me once you're twenty you're pretty well through. Well, the thin ones like Ruthie, maybe, they can keep going a while. But I'd like to see some of them down by the well try to make it. Even the ones with their husbands still alive, you can bet they wouldn't pay for it. They pay for me and I know what makes it happen to them and that means, ladies, that means: I know who they are. Eagh, what a stench, how can they live like this? Barely the skin for their bones. And all the ones on the boats and their fathers with the long beards, they pray and they give charity and they wear their shawls and read their scroll. I know who they are, ladies, when they weep and snivel, naked, for a little pain or when they want me to make like a little girl and then bend over. Oh, eagh, right in the gutter, look at that. Big holy men, ladies, and they let this go on. But glad to be away from that smell, how can they. . . ? Here we are, wonder if . . ."

She enters the tavern. She thinks: "No. Upstairs, sleeping.

Won't mind if I filch a cup of wine, though, helps me sleep. Samuel, there's a man, never bothers you. Except when he wants it and then it's in, out, thank you, Mary, no big fuss, like the others, like they have a wild stallion tied to their short hairs and it's dragging them along, must be a fine feeling even if you do make an ass of yourself."

She climbs the stairs to her room. And she thinks: "Rotgut he sells. Ha. Tied to a stallion, really. And they don't have robes like these, those old cunts, who'd give them to you, and these bracelets, and look, bitches, how firm they stand, soft. Tied to a stallion and riding the beautiful ladies with their soft softnesses here and here and there where you can burrow and warm. Good to lie down. Good wine rotgut. Up into them, into them, where the life of the dark is . . ."

She sleeps.

5. The Collector's Journal continues, containing the third poem in the Jesus cycle.

When Jesus arrived at Bethabara, he found John preaching to a large multitude. The fiery red-beard stood waist-deep in the water and shouted up at the bank where pilgrims and acolytes sat crowded together, listening. At once, Jesus became excited.

"Prepare your heart for *metanoia*!" John cried. "For I cleanse you with water, but it will cleanse you as with a flame. Prepare yourself for *metanoia* with every action, for *metanoia* is every action. And do not seek in scripture or in this rule or that rule. Do not say: I am God's chosen. God can raise his chosen from the stones. With this water, cleanse your heart of every conception. Of the evil and of the good. Look upon your neighbor whom you despise and say, 'I am that man,' until your heart is clean of every opinion of right and wrong. Prepare your heart for *metanoia*."

When Jesus heard this, he knew he had found the teacher he was seeking. He approached John and asked to join his community. John was immediately convinced of the man's serious intention and admitted him.

So Jesus became a neophyte at the monastery of John, and this was, perhaps, the happiest time of his short life. He was enthralled with the Baptist; hung on his every word—and those words seemed to lend a special importance to the most trivial events. Where once Jesus had derided his father's profession and called it lowly, he now labored cheerfully as the monastery's carpenter. Now, the joining of a barrack's lintel, the repair of a cistern—like planting the communal fields or unloading the tools from a pack mule's back or rubbing his flesh with olive oil to keep off the sun—these things seemed infused with John's preaching. They were part of the preparation of his heart for *metanoia*.

Soon, Jesus stood once again by the banks of the Jordan as the Baptist, half-submerged, cried out his message. This time, Jesus was nervous, trembling like a bride. He had come to be baptized.

One of a small line of believers, he slowly descended the banks. He stepped from the mud into the water. He waited while John lay his hands on the shoulders of each in turn, gently pushed each one down until only the believer's hair could be seen, just below the surface, waving in the current. John would let go. The acolyte would burst from the river, gasping. Jesus would move forward, closer to John. His baptism is the subject of the next poem in the collection:

In love with the reflected sun,
I wade into the river.
My white robe spreads on the surface like a lily,
then dampens as it sinks until it clings about my legs.
The Baptist's are a workman's hands:
They push me down.
The river is not torn as I descend:
The dense bushes mirrored by the water rend
and ripples from the rift bend the riverweeds
like women bending at a well
above a child. And I go under.

Somehwere there are hours leaning on a plough,
bored in the hot sun, stifled by desire,
mad with old arguments, and almost dead with dreaming,
but here the flow becomes me.
I am the Baptist below and he above me
plants me in what I am that I might rise—
out of the labyrinth of days and of deciding,
out of the river and the life that ends
into the sun, and the life everlasting.

PART II: THE CALL

1. The Collector's Journal continues.

After his baptism, Jesus moved into the inner circle of the Bethabara community, and impressed many, including John, with his intensity of feeling. He now became acquainted with Simon, a young fisherman's son of Capernaum in Galilee. Simon lived in the community with his wife, Sarah. He was a small, hawk-faced, nervous man, but even then, he showed himself a shrewd thinker with a turn for politics. He and Jesus became friends at once. And many evenings when the day's work was done, the two could be found bent together over the last of the lamplight, their bodies cloaked in darkness and their eager gazes etched in flame, as they engaged in earnest discourse on the sayings of their master. For instance, when John had preached against the raising of the eagles above the temple, Simon said to Jesus:

"It seems to me that the master is moving us toward action, and that he himself will soon be revealed to us as greater than we now know. If the actions of Pilate are sinful and we are the acquiescent, taxpaying wards of Pilate's government, haven't we partaken in sin to such an extent that the path of God will be closed to us? John acts in speaking, and, true, we speak through our presence, listening to him. But mustn't his speech progress toward the eradication of the evils he condemns—the desecration of the holy, the oppression of the weak? And, if so, mustn't our presence progress toward revolutionary action? Mustn't we risk even treason to bring *metanoia* to the people?"

But Jesus replied: "How, when you have been beneath the water, can you still deal in surface things? Hasn't the centurion come to John and said, 'How can I be saved?' And John said, 'Be a good centurion.' And the tax collector, hasn't he come, and John said, 'Be a good tax collector.' Where is the condemnation in that? John will not change the heart of Rome because Rome has no heart nor of the Jews because the Jews have no heart. Only each man has a heart, and when John attacks the eagles above the temple, it would be best to ask yourself: What is the eagle above my own holy of holies, and to what do I pay homage when I might be attending to my soul? Who cares if a standard hangs above a building when your soul is in chains? And what more radical act is there than to seek within for your soul's freedom?"

"Then you are like the priests," Simon said, "who interpret every word spoken to them so that it conforms to their image and demands no action of them."

And Jesus said: "Then you are like the Zealots, who cast out sin by committing murder."

And so the debate continued until everyone around them was confused and went to bed. Yet it was not an idle argument and was now to play a part in matters of life and death.

At that time, the tetrarch of Galilee and Peraea was one Herod Antipas. He was a tyrant, this Antipas, but he was also a slave; that is, he ruled according to his passions which, in turn, ruled him. He was an enormously fat man, whose labored breathing when he moved from bed to throne was as loud as his heavy footsteps in the marble halls of his palace. His jowls rippled down the sides of his childish, pouting face, his skin was pocked and broken, and both the hair on his head and that on his chin were sparse, having fallen out from excess and poor diet. But neither these facts nor anything else could deter him from satisfying his appetites.

Herod's wife was the daughter of Aretas and Aretas was the king of Arabia. But Antipas had recently traveled to Rome, where he had met his niece Herodias, the wife of his half-brother Philip. Herodias was beautiful. Her figure was lush and her black hair rode on the roundness of it to her waist. She had the full lips and the dark eyes of a born lover. But what she loved was power. She had long despaired of gaining that power through her honest husband. So when she saw Antipas, she forced down her disgust at his enormity and set about seducing him. This was not difficult. Antipas was such a man that she had only to run her tongue once or twice along the folds of his chins, whisper to him that he might some day become a king—and he was hers.

Soon, Antipas' wife was informed by her spies that her husband was planning to divorce her. She formed a plan of her own. Upon his return, she sweetly requested that she be allowed to travel to their fortress at Machaerus for a vacation. He, with the true stupidity of those who believe themselves cunning, agreed. The moment she was gone, he gleefully beckoned Herodias to join him at his palace. Unfortunately for Antipas, his wife also acted quickly. No sooner did she reach Machaerus, than she slipped across the border to Arabia to inform her father of the shame that was to be brought upon her. Aretas ordered his armies to mass on the Arabian plains.

A messenger went forth from Machaerus to the palace of Antipas. He found Antipas stretched naked on his couch, looking every bit like a swine washed ashore three days after drowning. Were it not for a filmy sheet which covered the tetrarch's loins, his faithful servant would not have been able to overcome his nausea and approach. Even so, the stench of wine which rose from Antipas like miasma almost overcame the good man. At last, however, the messenger stepped forward, and said, "Tetrarch, Aretas is calling for revenge. He is planning an attack on Machaerus." Antipas, lying on his side, his head resting on his hand, nearly fell over as he jerked himself from a snooze. "Oh no!" he said. "What? Oh no. Oooh. Ooooh, I hate this country." And he tumbled to his feet, shouting for his troops to prepare for a march to the fortress.

Now, one evening shortly after these things had come to pass, John the Baptist was sitting at dinner with a number of his acolytes—among them, Jesus and Simon. And John stood up before them.

"I've decided to go to Machaerus to preach against Antipas," he said simply. "The tetrarch has committed incest by marrying his brother's wife."

When Jesus heard these words, he jumped to his feet, overturning his bowl so that the white curds splayed across the table.

"Rabbi, if you go to Machaerus," he said, "the people will think you are another politician come among them to win power."

But Simon was excited and, almost at the same moment, he said: "Now, for the first time, the people will see you as you are."

John looked at his two disciples, first one, then the other. He grinned. "One would turn God into History, and one would turn History into God," he said. "But I'm afraid both will interpret me to myself until I disappear completely."

At that, Simon was humbled and fell silent. But Jesus was

heartsore because he felt he had been rebuked for his understanding.

The next day, John set out, accompanied by his followers. It
was then the rainy season, and the Baptist strode through the
downpour, his staff in his hands, while the others struggled
along behind him. When they reached the fortress, they had to
climb a steep and muddy trail, but John was not deterred. He
trudged upward, his red hair plastered to his scalp, his staff
digging fiercely into the wet earth. He never looked back.

Finally, the group came before the fortress itself. They
gathered in the rain beneath the black wall that loured against
the black sky. Running soldiers and rearing horses and heavy
mulecarts filled with arms were rushing everywhere, churning
up the mud.

John stood before the fortress and began to shout.

"Why are you going to war, my people? Because Antipas has
committed incest? Will you murder and die on the plains of
Arabia because Philip's wife is an incestuous whore? Oh, my
people, my people, the flesh is twisted. The flesh is twisted till
the flesh is torn and the path of God is made into a battlefield.
Antipas has begot murder on the body of his brother's wife.
Murder and death on the plains of Arabia. Antipas *is* murder:
His incest is become the dying armies of the plain! Turn back!
Prepare in your heart the way of the Lord!"

As John preached, Jesus listened in horror. He feared for the
great man's life. The others, too, were amazed that John could
say such things and not be arrested at once. But John preached
all that day and into the night in the rain until his voice was
hoarse, and the sound of beasts and carts and splashing mud
and water drowned him out completely. And yet, he stood

43

there still, preaching on. Large crowds of people gathered around him to listen and watch. The gray sky grew light again, and still John stood as one inspired or possessed and shouted at the fortress wall.

Now, in Antipas' entourage there was a steward named Chuza, whose wife, Joanna, had been baptized by John. When daylight came, Joanna snuck out of the fortress. Wrapped in a shawl, she approached the Baptist and spoke to him quietly.

"You are in danger, John," she said. "All night long, Antipas has sat in the marble throne in the great hall, wondering what to do. He's afraid if he arrests you, there'll be a riot among the people, and when his army is occupied with that, Aretas will attack. But Herodias is a proud woman, and she's furious that someone like you should be allowed to insult her in public. She's dumped enough wine into the tetrarch to fill even him, and she's fed him on truffles, which he loves. And, also, though I blush to tell you, she has played with him in the most outrageous ways until he grunts like a camel and can be heard throughout the hall. Then she denies him, saying she could not sleep with a man who permits his wife to be denounced as a whore in the street. Antipas would never act on his own. He just sits in his chair saying, 'Ooooh, I hate this country,' over and over. But that woman has brought him to the boiling point. Run for your life."

The Baptist smiled at Joanna, who was both beautiful and mild. He reached beneath her cowl and laid his palm upon her fair hair, and she bent her head against his hand and held it in her own. John looked at her sadly. Then, clutching his staff more firmly, he lifted his face, and shouted hoarsely up at the fortress:

"Antipas is committing incest and so the armies are going to war! Turn back. Prepare your heart for the way of the Lord."

Joanna turned from him and ran, the rain and the tears mingling on her cheeks. Even as he shouted, John watched her until she was once again out of sight within the fortress.

John went on in the same manner throughout the morning. Afternoon came, and he went on, and the sky grew even gloomier as the rain poured down, and the fortress loured above. Finally, slowly, the gates of Machaerus groaned and opened. John faltered and fell silent. For a few seconds, the steady patter of the rain was the only sound. Then, another patter seemed to rise up under the first, blend with it, and finally overwhelm it: It was the sound of men marching.

A contingent of about twenty soldiers, led by a lieutenant, came parading out of the fortress. They looked neither left nor right. They just came on until, at a shouted order from their leader, they halted directly before John.

The lieutenant was a tall, lean man with sharp eyes in a hardbitten face. He stared at the Baptist. The Baptist returned the stare. He smiled at the lieutenant. The lieutenant returned the smile. Then the lieutenant drew his sword and raised it across himself.

The Baptist shouted: "Turn back! Prepare in your heart the way of the Lord!"

The lieutenant brought the flat of the sword down on the side of John's head.

The towering prophet stood another moment as if he would continue preaching as before. But at last, he swayed this way and that—and toppled over like a tree into the mud.

Jesus cried out and started to run forward, but Simon rushed to him, restrained him. The whole crowd surged toward where the Baptist lay. The lieutenant turned one long gaze upon them all. One gaze—and they stopped, and fell back from him.

The lieutenant gave a command and his soldiers trotted to the fallen preacher. They took hold of him under his armpits, and began to drag him away. With a final insolent glance at the frozen multitude, the lieutenant himself turned his back on them and strode to the head of his contingent. Dragging the Baptist with them, the soldiers entered the fortress and vanished from sight.

Not until the gates had thundered shut did Simon release his hold on Jesus. When he did, Jesus sank down on his knees in the mud and there continued to cry out and weep until his friends removed him from the place.

2. The Tale of Mary Magdalene continues.

Mary is in her bed in the upstairs room of the tavern. And she thinks: "What would he why am I thinking of him? But then what would he think if he saw me now? But he must know, imagine, why am I but he must. What with this fat bum fucking my fat bum and and me squealing fuck me hit me and him slapping my ass grunting like a galley crew he can hardly breathe and the foul farts from the fish he eats like a whale opening his yaw to suck it in well it's all faking but would he turn his back and walk away? Would he lunge . . . ah God, the weight of him. If he'd let me put a pillow under my belly but he wants me on my knees with my rear high God knows half the time what they're thinking but would he lunge and deck him giant that he is and rip his balls off bloody with that irongentle hand and take his place behind and fuck me beat me for my badgirl sins? Why, and him a drunkard, do I think of him? It's getting on my nerves, it's getting so I watch the door and worry where I am when he might see me and fuck him for what he did. Would he? Lunge, deck, rip, fuck, beat . . . oh no, not with this fat fart I won't. Think about . . . anything: the colored tents of Jericho. If Nicka had been his size, the drunkard's size, then my father . . . Well, I could've used him then with his chiding eye and his swagger and the smell of wine when he leaned over the table to me with those two wine sellers falling back into their seats just the way he looked at them. Shit, he's getting rough and that hand the size of an oar. Big, big man. All of them. The drunkard too. Big men, the lot of them, with women they buy. Cowards. The two of them, picking up their stools, falling back, and he picked me out like that, bold, to just come up with the two of them sitting there buying the wine biding their time waiting their turn. It was an evil night, all around, after the two Romans came, as if they hadn't their own taverns. Just to start trouble they know they're not supposed to. Centurions. Not even here for the girls which I could understand they could tell their comrades what a Jewish piece is like, but they just tromped in with the sound of their boots on the floorboard and not even taking off their helmets with their plumes waggling and their capes billowing and the flash of cuirass in the torchlight. Just stood the two of them and downed their wine three gulps apiece with every yellow fisherman trying not to fall silent around them, and then wiped their mouths with the backs of their hands and wiped the room with their insolent eyes and settled on me as if they were thinking about it and just to let the boys know they could if they wanted and then flung their filthy money down for Sam to chase across the bar and turned and tromped out and we heard their shouts and the horses galloping away. Oh, the fat fuck, is he, yes, slowing down, trying to stretch out his few shitty pieces of silver. Oh, let him have his night tonight long as he doesn't crack me another one like that I'll let him know it and he won't fuck with me once I do because I know what he is and he knows I know because they stick their secrets up me and then I have them up there until I let them out. Does he have them, I wonder? Secrets? The drunkard, with his swagger and his chestnut hair and eyes and the smell of his wine and his Roman scars? The way he came in after that . . . It was evil after that, after the Romans left, like they'd left a fog behind, rage it was. I could look around and see it. The skinny one in the corner still trying to sing with the red wine spilling bloody into his beard and his three friends with him pounding their palms on the table in time and all of them with the whites of their eyes bugging, staring desperate at the sound of the song and the hands pounding as if it could wipe away how those conquerors stared at me. And I'm thinking: I'll be the one to get it tonight, they'll take it out on me for certain. I'll be Pontius Pilate to them tonight and they'll ram me like galleys till they feel like men again. And I'm sitting with those two who were wine merchants a minute ago, hoping for a little extra for their trade, and now all of a sudden they're warriors telling me their sad, half-baked stories of what they almost did to some Roman who stopped them on the road . . . when just then he comes in weaving drunk and sees me bringing them another jug and stares and I thought, fuck you, sweetie, wait your turn like a good boy. But he didn't, came right over and leaned down with the smell of his wine and asked me if I'm free. And the two of them, the merchants, well, the whole place stopped when their stools turned over as they jumped to their feet, and every hopeful eye was on them to start a brawl and wash the Roman taint away. And then the drunkard waited for them. Just that. Just stood straight and easy—God, he's a giant— and waited for them to make their move. And they made their move all right: they picked up their stools and sat down again and stared into their wine. I don't know why I said yes except I did. If he saw me now. Pound this fat fuck's face like he is fat fuck pounding my cunt, and give him a cunt of his own, rip

49

them off for him and then set to me to show me badgirl . . .
oh, I have to stop, really, I won't with this humping camel.
Usually don't let a man kiss me on the mouth, don't know
why I did. Sometimes Samuel after he's taken it out of me for
something and I know it'll get him up and Ruth sometimes I
let when I'm feeling sad, but it was the way the drunkard
looked at me. If he'd smirked, I swear, like they do, when I
stared at that prick the size of a column but he just looked on
at me solemn-like and I made out I was looking at the
purpledark, jagged scar up the side of him and I'm looking, I
guess, for the secret, and I say, 'You're a wanted man, then.'
And he says, 'Not by many.' 'And a drunk now and then,' I say.
'Always,' he says. 'A rebel,' I say, 'cause I want to see him
shiver, and he's not even afraid, he says, 'No. But I was.' So I
say to him, sort of spitting it, 'cause I don't like the way he
keeps looking at me, 'How if I tell the next centurion? For
some extra change? I'm a whore, ain't I?' And he smiles; smiles
and says, 'Shit. I wish I'd known that before I took you home
to Mother.' And I . . . Here he goes. About time. If I call him
Daddy now he'll flood like a dam breaking. . . . tried not to
laugh but he saw me smile and his eyes changed like something I'd never seen . . . or Nicka . . . like me smiling lit him
up inside, all fiery, and he took my shoulders and before I
knew it, it was before . . . he kissed me, tongue so warm like
Ruth's tit, soft, deep, or cock when it's sweet like when Samuel
forgives me and makes me go down. Had to gasp out of it, that
kiss. 'Don't do that.' And he did it again that column pressing
up against me, thought he'd rip me with it. But he didn't
before it was before I knew it he was in me gentle and hard and
his hands on my shoulder never had one since I been here not
one do me that way like I really mattered, tongue in my

mouth, hands over me, cock so far up in me feeling full, pregnant with it and I start to fake it and then it comes on me never before except when Ruth gives me clitlick and I even fight it except I don't want to fight it screaming oh God here he comes and I'll, have to stop thinking that drunkard God I want to oh fat fucking shithead have his balls for lunch I want to oh Daddy now, sweet, fuck, beat, Daddy, oh . . . oh . . . shit . . . mad, going mad, can't stand it, must be oh what a mess must be mad shit, god, like I'm . . . oh, I hate that bastard, that drunkard what he did to me. I knew it, knew it."

3. The Collector's Journal continues, containing the fourth poem in the Jesus cycle.

Jesus returned with Simon and the others to the monastery at Bethabara and there awaited news. News did come, but it was only this: The forces of Antipas and Aretas had met on the Arabian plains, and, after a brief struggle, Antipas' army was reduced to nothing. Aretas had thought better than to press an invasion on a tetrarch protected by Rome. He considered his vengeance complete and his insult answered and he returned home with his daughter, leaving Herod to enjoy his new bride, and she to enjoy his new powerlessness.

There was much discussion of these events at Bethabara. Many of the monks saw them as a sign of God's wrath and looked forward to the eventual release of the Baptist by supernatural means. Others feared that Antipas, in his embarrassment, would unleash his rage on John and kill him. Simon said that pride would prevent Antipas from releasing John while military weakness would prevent his risking a riot by killing him. So until Antipas resolved his dilemma, Simon said, they could only wait.

Jesus did not take part in these discussions. By day, he worked in silence about the monastery or in the fields. By night, as the rains abated, he sat alone on the barracks rooftop and stared at the stars. Such a vigil is described in the next poem in the collection:

Son of Man

With lamplight and darkness breathing in turn
in the crags of his cheeks and brow,
he told us stories:
the hunched mother weeping in the door;
the small, then smaller figure of a young man journeying
who would come to great halls that yawned before him,
frescoed, and thick as mourning in the throat
with incense, and purple-bursted fruits
and cracklin' drooling on a roasted pig.
And some reclining princess there would brand
the rise and falling of her hip upon his fingers
till he reached for her;
then wind from the suddenly opened door
would make the fire dying in the grate
rear like a beast on the contortions
of the face that discovered them;
and you could almost feel the shackles
corrode his ankleskin and wrists
until they scraped red bone.
Someone always rescued him—his father or
the girl he'd left behind—
stomaching over dungeon flags in the dark
with a sword or a key.
And he faded into bedtime glad
that the dew cool grass would sometimes overcome
a sweat like crystal hung on the shoproom air;
the dew cool grass I remember.

My skin is crawling. The air's like a leper now:
wildflowers on the wilderness wind

sick with dung and the heat.
Why is the voice of my dead father in my mind tonight?
his fabricating rage against his sons
still spinning stories like a hunter after dinner,
on and on, unchanging as the stars, and the star stories
that mince your vision into constellations:
of a hero with a head like a cinderstone
thwacking the scales from the humps of a kraken
fanging the cloakcurve of a farmer pressing
his stupid yellow callus to the handle of a plough.
Who made the stories of the stars, anyway?
Which of the rich who cheat,
which of the poor who steal,
which of the kings who kill,
which of the slaves who follow death
had the gall to print his miserable imagination on the sky?

If I could fix my eyes upon the night,
I would carry a child on my shoulders into it,
show him where the constellations are erased
by light's simple incessancy. I would tell him:
Nothing's still where there is silence:
It's the business of the darkness to revolve;
up here, not to journey is a kind of dying.
And what, then, would he make of me?

But, of course, I can't.
I mark the time. I'm scared.
In the dark beneath the stars like stones,
I mark the time here,

hungry, hungry, hungry not to die.
Not to get sick and die young,
not to grow old and die.
Not even to stretch my fingers toward
the limit of eyes not even upturned
for fear of dying in the unwritten desire,
dying in the big quiet
and the passion to speak myself
into the symbol of this sadness.

The weeks passed without word of John. Some lost their courage, others lost their faith, and these drifted back to their homes. Still others, who would not go, gathered together to discuss how to govern the monastery in the Baptist's absence.

After one such meeting, Simon came to Jesus where he sat on the barracks roof. The two were silent there for a long moment, Simon standing and staring out upon the dark wilderness, Jesus, seated, staring up at the stars. Then Simon spoke angrily.

"They are already trying to turn John's word into a doctrine—into a stone which will sink within their minds until it's forgotten. They've already made John a saint so that they need only praise him without listening to him. My wife and I are leaving this place, my friend. We are going to return to our home in Capernaum. My brother Andrew writes to me that many there are hungry for the Baptist's good news, and believe his words can deliver them from their unhappiness. Come with me, Jesus. There is that in you which is not in me, which the people will recognize. And Sarah says that when you speak you have a power among the women. Neither of us can preach like John, but we can preach of John until he is released."

But Jesus, never removing his gaze from the heavens, said: "I'm leaving, too. I follow John not the followers of John. You'll do well to bring the word of *metanoia* to those who know you. I will also go to my home in Nazareth and speak to my own people."

So Simon and Sarah left for Capernaum, and a few days later, Jesus left for Nazareth.

When Jesus arrived home, his family celebrated his return, and he was glad to be with them. He sat with them in the evening and they brought him wine and he told them about John. At first, they listened to him. But as he went on in his excitement, his mother began to frown to herself. And finally she spoke with disdain.

"Well, I am only glad you have come to your senses and returned to your proper place," she said. "This wise man sounds like a fool to me for challenging Antipas in the open like that and risking not just his own life but also the lives of his followers."

"But if you don't die for something, Mother, you die for nothing," Jesus said.

At which point, Joses spoke up, and said: "Oh, it's easy to die for some false messiah and leave the real work to others."

Jesus nearly trembled in his anger at these remarks. But he kept his tongue. He rose and left the house. He went into the workshop and stood there alone in the growing dark. When James found him, he was contemplating a mallet hung on the wall.

Jesus looked up at his younger brother. "I went away to become a man," he said. "I have not returned to become a child again."

Now, not long after this, Jesus was invited to read in the

synagogue. The rabbi wanted to welcome him home and to hear about the famous John.

When the Sabbath day came, Jesus was nervous. He stepped into the dark place after the congregation was seated, and walked between the benches with his head down until he reached the front. There, with the candlefire from the menorah dancing on his earnest face, he read this verse from the prophet Isaiah:

The Spirit of the Lord is upon me; he has appointed me;
He has sent me to announce good news to the poor
to proclaim release for prisoners,
and recovery of sight for the blind;
to let the broken victims go free,
to proclaim the year of the Lord's favor.

When he had done, he rolled up the scroll and returned it to the attendant. The congregation watched him and he swept his eyes over their faces—faces familiar to him since his childhood.

At last, in a loud voice, he said: "Today, in your hearing, this prophecy is fulfilled." Because he had come to announce the words of John, who had brought freedom and the good news of *metanoia*.

As Jesus again scanned the congregation, he saw the people staring back at him. At first, there was silence. Then, all at once, the people began to laugh. They laughed and they murmured. Jesus could hear them. From the women's gallery, he could hear one farmwife leaning toward another, saying: "Who does he think he is now, I wonder?" And the second answering: "He still looks like Joseph the carpenter's son to me." And then a third behind them: "He left his brothers to support his widowed mother and now he returns a prophet, is that it?" The laughter continued. Wealthy merchants in the front row chuckled. Jesus heard one say: "I don't know about you, but I remember when he soiled himself at Succoth as the women danced." "Yes," said another, "and how his father beat his bum with a stick for chasing a cat with an awl." Jesus could hear them all and he could hear their laughter. And it was even worse when the laughter subsided, because there Jesus stood alone, with his face flushed and the wet, merry eyes of his neighbors peering at him.

The rabbi, his cheeks red with suppressed laughter, thanked him, and Jesus stepped down. He hurried up the aisle as he had come, his head lowered, looking neither to the left nor the right.

He spent that afternoon in the fields at the edge of the village. He returned in the evening and stood outside his house a while, listening to the voices of his brothers and sisters as they ate their supper. They were laughing, too. The laughter stopped as Jesus came through the door. Standing before them grave and erect, he announced he would once again be leaving.

And before the sun came up, he was on his way to Capernaum.

4. The Tale of Mary Magdalene continues.

Mary sits in a patch of high grass and flowers at the edge of the village. And she thinks: "What is that? What is that? God. Nervous. Nervous. Gutshivering inside all the time now, waiting. What is that? For him to come in: the drunkard. Catch me. Dust. Someone coming. Far on the horizon. Shimmer of dust on the grassy plain. Gets so I can't keep my mind on. Even here where I can sometimes come. The lilies drooping, swaying in the little breeze like sad ladies on the shore and the purple violets flung wide as if for the ships' returning. Stomach so nervous. The runs. I'm a held breath. Waiting for him to come, he never comes, to see me, see me like I am. As if he thought I were a virgin and he didn't know. I keep thinking he'll beat me, kill me maybe. What is that out there? Bad dreams. Dreamed about Nicka in an open grave. I'll kill you, she said, before I see you go off with him. My own mother. He's a Greek, I'll kill you. And it wasn't that, either. It was that he was a man, with a Greek cock that stood up and she couldn't stand me getting it because the rabbi hadn't touched her, probably, in years. Women old. Women trying to hang on to the parts of them that tore out, grew away. Don't you wish they could stay like that, the mothers saying to each other. Pretty strange it would be if they did. You think they're trouble now wait'll they start walking, they say. Wait'll they start fucking, they mean. Wait'll you dry up and die, I'll kill you. She says. And the old fat man without his own mind she

61

gives him the two-fingered goose and he jumps up screaming for her, standing over me with his beard flowing white and his face turning red. Well, sure, Daddy doesn't like thinking about Nicka's rod up me either, or even that I bleed, or have hair on me or that I'm not sitting on his lap again under the white and green striped tent bright with the sunshine and him telling me after little Jacob died the stories of the Maccabees as if I were a son to him when little Jacob, little Jacob died. Wants me like that again. Has me set up with a fox-faced scribe with skin that looks like the moon so he can still be the only man in my . . . Oh, the way my stomach feels, like it's my time again already. But I'll bet more shit than blood comes out of me, don't know why I should bleed anymore if I'm unable. Unfair. They get to stand up and we bleed like dogs waiting for them to stop the bleeding like dogs, panting for it from them. With Nicka in the orchard and trees ever-so-black in the silver light of the moon, ever-so-full. I bled then. Like they start you bleeding, and then you have to pant for them to stop it. All of him dark, except for his eyes, sparking with the moon. What is that? Getting bigger. Like a long line of dust now. Must be coming this way. Shadows in it. Men. Soldiers? Oh, oh, mama, I don't want to be a whore anymore. Right. Shit. What, then. Once he stopped it. Started it and stopped it with the same fifty strokes of his sweet, thick Greek cock—couldn't have been more than that, fifty, but it was his dark, dark eyes burning white, white with the full silver moon and the black trees hanging up there behind him and oh, I was pregnant all right, and what an idiot to go to them, trusting, mama, what do I do, papa? But not for the rabbi of Jericho, the priest of Jericho. Lucky he didn't have me stoned. Lucky to escape with my life. Nicka lucky to get away. Meet me on the tailor's road in Jerusalem, he says. But there was only the old lady there, and no Nicka. Her and her potions. My stomach on fire. Like now. Waiting for him. Like waiting for that drunkard like he's going to come again, what did he do to me, don't want to be, don't want to be anymore, but where was I supposed to go, no money, bleeding, damn near died with it all pouring out of me, so much blood then. So much shit now. Lilies and violets and a cloud of dust. Definitely men, not soldiers either. Maybe the Baptist's people from Capernaum. Heard they were. Heard they don't. Whore. Don't. Wouldn't it be funny? Daddy? Funny to find God, sweet, like his warm tongue in my mouth, not worrying if he comes, can't stand it, like going mad. And coming with that fat fart fucker, that was the end, the end. I hate, I hate. And Samuel saying: 'Well, what's wrong then?' like I'm supposed to, well I am, spread it for every and what if he sees? Oh God, sweet, look at me, oh, the rabbi, father, says even once, but God, only two years of it, I'm still only fifteen, forgive. Oh, they come on like dancing. Silhouettes in the cloud of dust. Of men together. Walking toward the hill. Grass to their thighs. Now the dust behind them, around them, like two hands carrying them to the hill. All the people following. Village people. I know them. Must be coming up from the sea road. Must be the people from Capernaum. The Baptist's people. Heard they don't. Women with them, too, then. Wonder if he's. What if I. But all the women from the village, they'd . . . And the men. Oh, I could tell those preachers a thing or two about their audience, maybe I will if anyone cracks a word. Look at it. Just like a dance, how they go up the hill. The whole crowd together, hazy still in the dust. And the people standing down in a ring at the bottom. And the rest walking up step by step. And some

63

more of them fluttering to the ground in a ring around the hill, and the rest, just a few of them now, just the Capernaum people I guess, going up toward the top. Now the rest—they go down to the ground like the flower petals when they fall. Then on to the top goes the one man."

Mary rises and moves forward through the high grass, joins those standing at the bottom of the hill. And she thinks: "I'll just. No one will. What does he look like? That man alone. Just a shadow, sky blue bright too bright, just the silhouette of him, arms out, welcome, have to move around, get the sun behind him there. Oh God. Wait. There. Oh God. God. Look at him. Look at his eyes. Never saw anything. Look at his eyes. Black hair all tangle-jaunty on his brow. Massy black curls tumbledown to his shoulders. And the beak and the thick, red lips for kissing. But those eyes. Like tunnels, dark tunnels, dark into the. Sad. Oh, like he knows. What am I, what's the matter with me, it's all the same brimstone argle-bargle nonsense: Whore. Get out of my house, I have no daughter. Whore. And they all get to feel. And they all get to feel so fine. Like when the tavern closes and they all go out, chests puffed, so clean, forgetting, with me to remember for them, who they are, the filth of their true-to-God being spewed into me while they can wear their righteousness until it rises again. Oh, men can be so brutally dishonest with themselves. Condemning, feeling pure in their condemning, when the secret, the secret to *metanoia* is simple, John told us: all you need do is make no judgments, judge nothing, nor, then, will you be judged."

5. The Book of Judas continues.

When Judas had recovered from his wounds, he returned to Magdala by stealth because the Romans had established patrols to capture him and the other rebels. And he lived as a fisherman again. But he was sad in his heart for the death of his friends.

At about this time, Abraham died too, and Naomi also died of grief for him. And Judas buried them and sang the prayers for them. And he said:

"I have left the womb but once,
but twice, I have buried my mother.
Once I have been created:
Twice I have laid my father in the ground."

And Judas began to drink. And Judas drank and drank. And Judas drank wine until he was drunk. And Judas drank every day until he was a drunk. And he drank so that he was a drunk among drunks. And many said of him: He is even a drunk of drunks. And still, Judas drank.

And Judas drank when he was fishing, so that he returned home with his nets empty. And his inheritance became small, and he could not pay his workers. And even so, Judas drank.

Now on one night, Judas was stumbling through the town. And he was drunk. And many women shouted at him from their homes because he sang loudly in the streets. And he sang:

Son of Man

"How do you make an emperor?
That's the song I sing.
The mater and the pater
of the present imperātor
had a night of fun that only later
turned into a king.
So, if he can put a Roman
in his noble wife's abdomen
who'll use Caesar as cognomen
and will wear the regal ring,
then to me it surely seemus,
if I Romulus her Remus
I could make a king with every little fling.
So I think I'll tell Sejanus
he can stuff it up his—ain't it so:
To make an emperor's an easy thing.

O, how do you make an emperor?
That's the question deep.
It cannot be that serious
to fashion a Tiberius
who half the time's delirious
and half the time's asleep.
If I find a queen and tease her,
and before old Julius sees her
I can squeeze her and then please her
till I've rammed the castle keep,
then the god I'll make is just as good
as ever great Augustus could
and probably not half as big a creep.

66

So I think I'll tell Sejanus
he can stuff it up his—ain't it so:
To make an emperor's an easy thing."

And when he had done singing, he found he was outside the town. And he saw before him a roadside tavern, and he went in there thinking to have more to drink. And the tavern was called Samuel's.

And Judas entered the tavern and looked about him. And he saw a harlot there, seated at a table with two men, and she seemed to him to be very beautiful. And his loins were stirred because of her beauty and he grew breathless and said:

"Her hair is long and silk and sable.
Her eyes are deep as pools and black.
Her skin, that is white as alabaster,
is soft as her breasts are soft and full.

I will lie on her as if she were the water:
I will lie like the reflection of the sky.
I will go into her like dawn into the night.
She is so beautiful, and will not deny me."

And Judas approached the harlot and asked her to lie with him. And she consented and stood and led him by the hand to her room.

And her name was Mary.

And Judas lay with her, and took great pleasure from her, saying in his heart:

Son of Man

"There is a wilderness within me where my cheek would lie
on this warm breast and travel in this silken cleft forever.
Honey of the lips of sadness, breath like wine,
my body made into her cries:
She is so beautiful and does not deny me."

And yet Judas hardly spoke, nor did he tell her his name.
And Mary stared at him, but was also silent.

And Judas arose and left the tavern. But the harlot remained
in his thoughts for many days. And Judas drank.

Now, one night, when he was very drunk, Judas went down
to Lake Gennesaret. And he climbed aboard his boat and sailed
out to a lonely place in the water. And Judas sat in his boat and
the waves rocked him gently, and the boards of the boat
creaked. And Judas saw the shadows of the other fishing boats
far from him in the night and he heard the cries of the
fishermen coming to him from far away.

And he said: "My God, I love the sea."

And Judas laughed in the night alone, because he had fallen
in love with a harlot.

And Judas drank and squandered his inheritance. And he
came home from the sea each day with his nets empty until he
felt he must soon be a beggar in the streets. And his lust for
Mary oppressed him, because he had no money and feared she
would laugh at him if he returned to her.

And Judas sat beside his boat on the shore of Gennesaret, for
his boat was in great disrepair and could hardly sail. And he
drank wine from a skin. And he laughed bitterly in his heart
and said:

"Behold the aftervision of my life
which hovers in the air now that the life is gone.
I am the shadow that was once the sun
and shimmers, moves and fades: not even darkness."

Now, as he sat and drank, he heard voices and looked to see who was speaking. And he saw a group of strangers conversing with the fishermen on the shore. And Judas heard them speaking of John the Baptist, a great prophet of the Jews who had been arrested by Herod Antipas.

And Judas was drunk. And he spoke to the strangers out of his bitterness and said: "Where is your prophet now? He is in Herod's prison. This is a suitable messiah for the Jews!"

And one man stepped forward from the group and said to him: "I am Jesus, baptized by John."

And Judas spat on the ground before the man's feet and said: "Now you have also been baptized by me."

And there was a great uproar among the fishermen. And they shouted: "Do not speak with this man. He is a drunkard who will be a beggar in the streets. Return to us and tell us why you and your people have come to Magdala."

And Judas said: "Yes. Tell us why you and your people have come to Magdala."

And Jesus laughed loudly and said to Judas: "We have come looking for a place to stay, and if you will let us stay with you, I will fix your boat."

And Judas agreed. And Jesus rolled up his sleeves and called for tools to work with. And he set about repairing Judas' boat until it was seaworthy again and looked as if it had just been made.

And Jesus and his companions came to stay with Judas so that the people of the town spoke together and said: "They cannot be from John, for they consort with drunkards and lecherous men."

And every day before dawn, the companions of Jesus sailed out with Judas on his boat. For they were fishermen from Capernaum. And when they returned, Judas' nets were so full that they could hardly lift them. And Judas was seen at the marketplace selling his fish and great jars of their jelly. And the people saw that he had drunk no wine and said among themselves: "Truly there is some power in the men from Capernaum, for they have filled the empty nets of the fisherman and cured him of his drunkenness."

And Judas conversed with Jesus many times. And one day, Judas said: "Why do you seek for God when He has abandoned us? Everywhere we are conquered and oppressed. I myself was in Jerusalem when Pilate murdered dozens of men even as they were sacrificing for the Passover. And when I tried to repay him in kind, my people were slaughtered. And what was John's sin that God has allowed him to be put in prison?"

But Jesus said: "If these men were murdered while they sacrificed, surely God could not have been angry at them. Or what about those eighteen people who just died in Siloam when the tower fell on them: Were they greater sinners than anyone else? Your angry God and your sinners and your good: You are only seeing your own heart in the world. John has brought the good news of *metanoia:* Look into your heart until you see neither good nor evil, then you will be so like God, it will be as if you were his son."

And Judas said: "How then will evil be punished or good rewarded?"

And Jesus answered him, saying: "Look at the world you have made for yourself, Judas."

Now the next day, Jesus gave a sermon to the people of the town. And he stood atop a hill and spoke to them. And Judas was with him and stood on the hill among his companions.

And Jesus said: "You have heard it said that you should love your neighbors: Love your neighbors and hate your enemies. But John came saying: Love your enemies; bless those that curse you; do good to those that hate you; and pray for those who persecute you. Then you will be like children of God, who makes the sun shine on the evil and the good, and sends the rain on both the just and the unjust."

And there was an uproar among the crowd, and they shouted at Jesus, saying: "How can we resist evil then?"

And Jesus said: "Don't. If it strikes you on the right cheek, offer it the left cheek, too."

Then, some men who were drunk and rowdy lay hold of a harlot who had walked in among them to listen. And they said: "Should we not obey the law, rabbi, and stone this sinful woman?" And they were laughing.

And Judas looked down upon the harlot and saw that it was Mary. And he would have gone down the hill to her and fought with the men, but he heard Jesus say: "Yes, stone her. And the one who has never sinned gets to throw the first stone."

And the people laughed at the drunken men until they let Mary go.

When Judas saw this, he was amazed. And he walked away from the crowd and sat by the sea alone.

71

6. The Collector's Journal continues.

When Jesus arrived in Capernaum, Simon made him welcome at once. He took the Nazarene into his home: a small house in which he lived with Sarah and her mother Susannah, his brother Andrew and others of their family. Simon also gave Jesus work on his boats, and on the boats of Zebedee, whose sons, James and John, were Simon's friends.

These friends were soon Jesus' as well. They found him a hard worker and an amiable companion, and they admired him because he, like Simon, had been one of John's disciples. The women of Simon's house were also pleased with Jesus. He was a man who seemed to understand them, and he treated them kindly. Not long after his arrival, in fact, Susannah took sick—to the point where many despaired of her life. But Jesus nursed her with uncommon skill, and she soon recovered.

Now, Simon would frequently hold meetings at his house in which his circle would gather to discuss the sayings of John. Jesus naturally joined in these discussions and he was greatly respected for his understanding. Many others came, too. The meetings were especially popular with the town's young men because women were allowed to participate, and also because the meetings had a rebellious atmosphere in which many things were said against the religious authorities.

In Capernaum, as in the towns around, these authorities were the Pharisees. They and their lawyers determined what was and was not permissible according to Jewish scripture. Unlike the Jerusalem priests, whose interests lay in the rich

and the Romans, the Pharisees believed that the law was for all
people and so imposed many burdensome regulations upon the
common folk. These, Simon and his group disavowed as John
had taught them. Along with allowing women to attend their
meetings, they also invited all manner of men: tax collectors,
drunks, mad beggars off the streets: outcasts whom the Pharisees considered unclean or sinful. They also held meetings on
the Sabbath, which the Pharisees considered strictly a day of
rest. And so they showed themselves defiant.

Old men, men of convention, ever fearful of the young, the
Pharisees began to worry about Simon and his people. They
conferred with the Herodian authorities to decide whether or
not the meetings were treasonous or heretical. But they were
afraid to condemn Simon publicly because he was associated
with John the Baptist, whom the people acclaimed as a
prophet. They murmured against the group, however. They
said their discussions were sinful and corrupted the young.
"John was a holy man who fasted and prayed and abstained
from wine," they said. "These men eat and drink and carry on
with the girls who hang around them."

When Jesus heard this, he laughed and said: "Yes, and when
John fasted and prayed and abstained from wine, they called
him a fanatic," a response which spread through the town
quickly, and silenced the Pharisees for a time.

Now, as his group became more popular, Simon began to
think about going out into the surrounding towns to bring the
word of John to the people there. So one day, as he was
mending nets with his brother, he raised the idea to Andrew.

And he said: "Now that John is gone, we would have to find
someone among us who could speak to strangers and appeal to
them. There are already too many messiahs in Galilee."

"Come to the point, brother," Andrew replied. "We both know such a man."

Simon looked troubled. And he said: "God sometimes lays a man's greatness in the brambles, where it calls to him to seek it if he will."

By this time, the Pharisees had grown very concerned over Simon's popularity. They now decided to invite him to speak in the synagogue on the Sabbath. They knew his ideas were radical, and they hoped he would condemn himself from his own mouth.

When Simon was told of the invitation, he saw his chance. He went in search of Jesus, and found the Nazarene sitting in the courtyard, watching the women at work.

"We are invited to speak in the synagogue," Simon said. "Will you be our spokesman?"

Jesus was surprised. "Why me?" he asked. "You're the leader of the group."

"I'm also skinny and nervous and funny to look at," said Simon. "And I have neither your insight nor your eloquence."

But Jesus said: "I spoke to my own people in my own synagogue at home and they laughed at me."

"John was laughed at, too, sometimes," said Simon.

At this, however, Jesus became angry. "I'm not John; I won't preach in John's place," he said.

Simon answered: "No. But if no one speaks up for us, we will seem to be afraid of the Pharisees. Then, even our own friends will desert us."

Jesus thought this over for a long time. But finally, he agreed to go.

On the night before Jesus was to speak, the Nazarene lay awake on his pallet for a long time. When at last he did sleep, he was restless. Once, in the night, he was disturbed by a dream which made him sit up shouting into the darkness. Susannah heard him, and came to his side.

And the woman said: "What was in your dream that terrified you so, my son?"

And Jesus answered: "Nazareth."

Simon was also awake in the dark. His wife Sarah lay with her head on his chest.

She whispered to him: "What if there is trouble in the synagogue, and the Herodians accuse us of treason?"

"Then we will have to leave Capernaum for a while," said her husband, "and bring the word of John to the towns around."

The Sabbath arrived. Simon and Jesus and their followers went to the synagogue. Even the women came. All of them stood before the impressive structure, sensing the weight of its authority. It sat by the sea, frowning toward Jerusalem, a building of dark basalt-stone with high windows and a pitched roof. A flight of steps swept up to a platform on which stone columns flanked the massive doors. The party entered through these doors and saw, within, the rows of columns that supported the women's gallery above and the rows of benches along the wall in which the men were sitting. The women went upstairs. The men took their places among the congregation. Jesus walked slowly up the center aisle between the columns until he stood before them all.

Once again, as in Nazareth, the eyes of the congregation were fixed upon him. He saw the Pharisees in the front rows with their long white beards lying across their interlaced fingers, which rose and fell in turn on their bellies as they breathed and waited.

These men had planned well. They had chosen a day on which Jesus would read verses concerning the holiness of the Sabbath, which Simon and his followers had disavowed.

Jesus read: "And the Lord spoke to Moses, saying: 'Speak to the children of Israel, saying, Keep my Sabbath, for it is a sign between me and you throughout your generations; that you may know that I am the Lord that sanctifies you. You shall keep the Sabbath therefore; for it is holy: every one that defiles it shall surely be put to death, for whoever works on the Sabbath, that soul shall be cut off from among his people.' "

Then Jesus looked up. He saw the smiles of the Pharisees framed in their white beards. He saw their bellies heave with sighs of satisfaction.

And he said: "Did God make man so that there could be a Sabbath? Or did he make the Sabbath for the benefit of man?"

That was all he said. The room was silent. The smiles of the Pharisees slowly faded. Jesus' questions could neither be answered nor condemned. The Nazarene began to step down from the pulpit.

And just then, someone started screaming.

His name was Jacob. He was a madman, who lived in the streets. Like other outcasts, he had come to the meetings at Simon's house; he had heard Jesus speak. He had come to the synagogue today in the grip of his delusions. Now, he stood from a bench in the rear, and shouted: "Leave us alone, Jesus of Nazareth!"

Every head turned toward him. He stumbled out into the center of the room. Simon and James grabbed him by the arms and fought to restrain him, but he pulled free and staggered toward Jesus where he stood.

He was screaming all the time: "What have we to do with

you, Jesus?" Then he stood still and gripped his face with his hands. "There are demons in me!" he shouted. "Demons!"

The congregation had risen as one. They stood as if made of stone, leaning toward the madman but fearful of approaching him.

Jesus approached him.

He lay his hand on Jacob's shoulder. He looked at him with eyes that seemed to glow until even the madman raised his face and met his gaze. And Jacob saw—and everyone in the synagogue saw—what Simon knew but none had fully seen before: the power of Jesus, the power of the man himself.

He spoke in a voice that seemed to shake the columns of the place.

"Be gone from him!" he commanded.

Jacob threw back his head and cried out—once. Then, blinking, he looked around him, his shoulders sagging. Finally, his eyes returned to Jesus, and they filled with tears. Jesus smiled.

"It's all right now, Jacob," he said softly.

But shouting erupted around the room. The Pharisees were enraged.

"Here are the followers of Simon!" they cried. "This is what they have made of the words of John."

Jesus faced them. His eyes still seemed to have a fire in them, and they all fell silent at his glance.

The people murmured: "Who is this man?"

One of the town fathers spoke out in a loud voice.

"By what authority do you speak?" he said.

"By what authority did John the Baptist speak?" said Jesus.

The man couldn't answer: either he must acclaim John a prophet or condemn him before the people. He trembled with rage, his white beard rippling. He pointed at Jacob and shouted: "This man is unclean!"

And Jesus answered: "He's clean now."

With which, the Nazarene turned his back on all of them, and walked through the crowd, out of the synagogue.

Immediately, the shouting erupted again, as some men spoke of Jesus with amazement and others condemned him at the top of their lungs. Among them all, Jacob stood still and wept.

And among them all, Simon clenched his fist at his brother. And he said: "Now. Now, we have begun."

7. The Tale of Mary Magdalene continues.

Mary is in her room above the tavern, and she thinks: "And I thought: now, he . . . Still, what am I doing? But I thought: now he will come down and tear them off me and fight them off me and say to me naughtygirl now take this this this with that column of his and me so filled with it it feels like bursting from my red mouth screaming. I thought: now, he . . . Funny, he should see me there finally. As if my father were to come upon me there of all the days and see me standing at a sermon. And him standing up there near the top of the hill and staring down at me sad, fierce; and sober, too. And when they grabbed me, I thought: now, he . . . But it was the preacher in the end. Maybe that's why I'm doing it. Still I must be crazy. Still, even when they were going after him, the preacher, with their questions, he was so calm and his eyes so laughing with the toss of his black hair, challenging them, almost like, sure, grinning to show off his good teeth and oh, they were after him. 'What if a man steals from you, don't you punish him?' And I thought: There's a point, I have to say the creep has a point, there's still right and wrong, you know, and he just stares them down, dares them down the tunnel of his eyes into the light, and bold as brass he says, 'Offer him all you own.' 'And if he attacks you, hits you?' they say, oh, they were after him, and he says, 'Offer him your other cheek to hit also.' And he's laughing at them. Your other cheek! In this neighborhood. Laughing at all of us. He had them riled, I'll tell you. I'll tell you what it was: they couldn't get him, couldn't confirm their miserable lives on him like they can at night on me. That's why they grabbed me, sure. Sure. And I thought: Now, he . . . the drunkard, standing up there, giant that he is, he's gonna come down after them so that the earth shakes with his steps and all I'll see is his face twisted red over me as he rams it naughtygirl into me and these two sons-of-bitches goddamn them with their hands all over me they'll be eunuchs then to serve me I can bend them over and give them a red-hot poker up the ass so they squirm and have to thank me for it, grabbing me, grabbing me like that, still have the bruises on my arms, look at them. And the spit's flying out of their broken teeth and out over their filth-braided beards and spattering onto my face and one of them's got me close to the breast and is kneading me in front of him like I'm a hunk of dough, and I knew the one of them, he'd been here, and I knew, I was ready to just shout out to them how he comes with his dick half limp—tell everyone. But I was afraid he'd kill me. And he would've too. I was afraid they'd all kill me with the drunkard and the preacher both of them looking on, and I prayed: Now, he . . . And they're laughing and shouting at me, eunuchs, 'What about her, Rabbi? Whores it at Samuel's down the road. Says right in the scripture we ought to stone her, don't it? Right in the books of Moses. Don't it? Should we stone her? Wouldn't go against the good book, would you, preacher?' Laughing. Grabbing me. Threw me to the ground. Threw me down into the dust like I was their spit they threw me. Pricks. And I just thought. It was just I thought. But it was the preacher in the end. With a voice like a fist or thunder. Never heard such a. Even my father when he threw me out. He says, 'Yes, absolutely. Stone her then.' And I thought: Oh, shit, I'm in big trouble now. 'Stone her then,' he says and then suddenly his voice dropping like just after the thunder and before the rain when the air's half green with pent-up lightning and even the birds stop singing and he says, 'but let him who has never done evil throw the first stone.' And I looked at the two of them tensed up over me, rising, angry, far into the air and their whole bodies clenched and I'm waiting, and I'm waiting, but the whole crowd is looking at them now, laughing at them, too, like he was, and they finally just waved their hands at him, waved him off, saying, 'Fuck him. Let's go get a drink.' And they were gone. And me laying there, not knowing where to look, eyes turning wild through a bracken of legs and sandals. And then slowly and then quicker they all started moving. The women first, the old women first and then the young, going off in a huff because he defended me. And then hoarse, coughing laughter of the men and then the men waving him off, waving him off and laughing and moving away. You'd think he'd. Well, something. You'd think he'd . . . mind. But he doesn't even and they're all walking away, laughing at him. He doesn't even mind. He saunters down the hill to me. Crouches down next to me with this comical look on his face and one eye screwed up, and sniffs a little and he says, 'So—who condemns you now?' And a bunch of others, the bunch that came with him standing in back of him, faces leaning in on me framed against the sky over his shoulder. God, I was shaking. 'No one, sir,' I said to him. And he nods and kind of looks off over the plain, scratches his nose, and then smiles down at me, says, 'Well—neither do I then.' And offers me his hand to help me to my feet just like that. And I get up, trying to dust myself off and put my hair straight and thank him and get the fuck out of there all at once: all those people looking at me, smiling like idiots. I'm trying. And the woman with them, Sarah, she says, 'Let me look at that.' The bruises. And she takes me aside. And I looked back for him, for the drunkard, and I thought: Now, he . . . But he was gone. Then. Gone. I wonder where he got so sober. Wonder what I'm doing, that's what I wonder should be wondering. I guess I'll take that. Probably need it. I don't suppose jewelry's not allowed, and hell anyway, fuck them telling me what. Anyway, I just may need it. All-right sort, this Sarah, the skinny one's wife, the nervous one, Simon. Nothing to say against her, it's not that. Plain face could use a little paint on her, but I saw some tough in her eyes and a nice pair she could make a living fix her up, not as nice as mine, wouldn't want to be her, having to answer to him, anyway, and her preaching at me, what the hell am I doing, I should just go down there go right down there and tell him forget it: go on without me. I'll take this. Oh yes. Wait'll they see me wear this they'll throw me out soon enough then I'll bet. Oh, sure, then, she says to me, Sarah, right out, says, 'You don't have to do this. You could come back to Capernaum with us. We have room.' Like saying, come to the table I'll buy you a drink, or let's go upstairs, easy as that. I said to her, I told her, it's not so easy, I said, 'Who's going to listen to you then with the likes of me aboard?' And she laughs, she just laughs. I think they're all insane. And I'm the insanest what am I doing? I wouldn't have. I told them. I said, 'You just go on and don't worry about me and thank you for your kindness but you just go on, thank you,' and that would've been the end of it, that would've been it. But then . . . But then, I'm sitting downstairs, I'm having some wine before Samuel wakes up, minding my own business, and there's a knock and I open it up, and there he is finally. It's him. The drunkard. Standing there. You could've blown me down. Standing there with a pack slung over his shoulder, just that, just a pack, and his fierce eyes, and his chestnut hair tangled down on his brow. And he runs his hand up through it and kind of looks off, like the preacher did, up toward where the highway starts and then he turns to me and I'm wondering whether to say We're closed or Come in when he just says 'I'm going with them.' Like that. Just 'I'm going' and at first I think so who cares what you do and then I realize what he means and I don't know what the hell I'm doing, I must be crazy, but I'm thinking, what the hell, there are taverns in Capernaum, too, right, can't be worse than this I'm thinking, and maybe there's something in it for the drunkard and me together, we could make a pair, if it comes to that, and I said, I must be nuts, that's all, don't want to cripple his mule anyway, no more will fit in it though I wouldn't mind filching that pillow with the swirls stitched into it, no, I'm nuts, but he just stood there like that, and I thought, what the hell, and I said. So I said. Well—I said: 'Wait up.'""

PART III: THE MISSION

1. The Collector's Journal continues, containing the fifth poem in the Jesus cycle.

After Jesus had spoken in the synagogue, the Pharisees began to preach more openly against him and Simon. Simon broached the subject now, and Jesus saw the wisdom of leaving Capernaum for a time. With money from Susannah's dower to assist them, they set out: the core of the group, including Andrew, James and John.

They traveled to nearby towns and many people came to listen to them and hear the teachings of John the Baptist. Frequently, it was Jesus who spoke: the incident in the synagogue seemed to have lent him a measure of authority over the others.

For several weeks, they stayed in Magdala. There, they met Judas Sicariot, and Mary the harlot, both of whom returned with them to Caparnaum.

They came home, finally, to find their renown had spread. The incident in the synagogue, the anger of the Pharisees and Herodians, the scandalous presence among them of Mary and other outcasts—all of these contributed to their notoriety. People now came to Simon's house forty and fifty at a time. Thieves and rebels sat beside honest and peaceful men, and even the scions of wealthy homes dared to come among them. Most of them were there to see Jesus, he who had defied both demons and Pharisees in the synagogue. They listened and

89

they spoke to him, told him of their troubles, tested their hidden rages against his understanding of John's word.

Soon, it was spoken all around the city that Jesus was a man of wisdom. They said he enlightened people with such skill and quickness that it was as if they had been blind before and now could suddenly see; that he freed them so in their actions that it was as if they had been lame and could suddenly walk.

As for Jesus himself, however, his friends could tell he was deeply troubled. His face was growing haggard, and his eyes sunken. When the people would leave Simon's house after a meeting, Jesus would sit alone, slumped and weary, as if—like the Jewish scapegoat—the sins of the city had been laid upon his shoulders. More and more often, he walked in the fields alone, or took a boat out on the lake. Sometimes, he simply sat in the courtyard watching the women work; the fifth verse in the collection deals with his reveries on one such occasion:

No wonder they chafe and snap through heatsplit lips
at all the little graspers at the ease within them;
puff in the shade of a ruddy el-bone,
swipe the hair-veins from their foreheads,
delve the embarrassment of their empty hands
into the making clean again.
Irritating to be the figment
of a child's desire or a man's,
to grunt while thudding at their hunks of dough,
or haul themselves from sleep to tend the lamps,
or heave the linen from the tubs
like flesh from the suction
of hunger, dark and nakedness—
and have it all glanced invisible

as if estates of labor traveled through them
while they just stood still, and still they stood:
exterior lines cascading from the light in their hair,
as from a notion of them, to the earth.

They feel it, too, though.
They haunt the songs that sing them swimming naked in a glade,
with someone approaching on the deadleaf bed,
and someone's thumb and index finger
parting the branches, and someone's eyes
wreathed in the stirless mosquitoes lining the underboughs.
Sometimes—sometimes you catch them: arching in the sun,
their fingers in their hair and their eyes closing,
and their red lips breathing apart
in a wild stopping of things.
Then they are what he sees
when even his bleakest season of adventure
glistens back out of the vanishing point
toward where they stand.
And then they bend again,
and their blouses sag
into a heat half gelled with flies;
And whatever is gone is beautiful among them,
and whatever is dreamed.

Now, one evening, during a meeting, Simon's house grew so packed with visitors that two beams of the roof had to be removed so that the people could listen to the discussion from the rooftop. When, finally, the crowd had left, Jesus spoke to Simon, Andrew and Judas. "Let's go out onto Gennesaret for a while and be alone," he said.

The four sailed out onto the water. Jesus sat by the rail, gazing overboard where the violet sky was shimmering on the waves.

Suddenly, he looked up at his companions.

"What are they saying about me?" he asked.

At first, no one answered. Then, Simon said: "They say you've taken up the mantle of Elijah."

Jesus was silent.

Simon had been thinking about the situation for a good while. He judged it was time to speak. "My friend," he said gently. "The moment has come for us to leave Capernaum again. For us to go out into the country—all over Galilee this time. For us—for you, Jesus—to speak to the people . . ."

But Jesus grew angry. He shouted: "You must think I wanted John arrested, or even murdered so I could take his place. Is that what they're saying about me? Is that what you say?"

Simon answered quietly: "I say you are John's words come to life."

"Oh no," said Jesus. "Oh no. I have had a dream, Simon: a dream in which I am standing on a rock high above the earth. And a man comes to me and he tells me that if I leap into the abyss he will make me fly. And he says he will turn the very stones to bread to fill my belly if I will follow him. And that he will give me kingdoms I can rule. And I resist him; and when I do, I suddenly see that he is the devil. And sometimes, Simon—sometimes, I think you are speaking to me in his voice."

Simon closed his eyes as if Jesus had struck him. But he persisted. "The fact remains," he said. "If we stay, we'll either have to disband or openly oppose the Pharisees and Herodians. If we give them an excuse, they'll jail us all, you especially. Up until now, you've passed through it in your confounded innocence like a man walking on the surface of a stormy sea. But when the storm overwhelms you, too, what then?"

And Jesus said bitterly: "Why have you so little faith? Has John abandoned us? Is he dead?"

"All right, then, we'll stay," Simon answered. "If any man can quiet the rising tide against us, you are the man."

Because Simon did have faith: but not in John.

And so, Jesus remained in Capernaum, and he remained despondent. Then came a day when things changed.

That day, Jesus was in the house speaking to a large number of people. Simon came close to him and whispered in his ear.

And he said: "Jesus, your mother and your brothers have come here to see you."

Jesus blanched. At once, he stood up and went outside. There, indeed, was his mother Mary, his older brother Joses, and his younger brother, James.

"The news has reached us that you preach here like a madman, making the authorities angry," Mary said to him. "Don't you remember what happened to your John? Are you really mad?"

Jesus stood before her, white and trembling.

"You neglect your family, Jesus," Joses said. "You're making us ashamed."

"We are going to take you home right now," said Mary.

James said nothing, but only stared at the ground.

Jesus was also silent. He was unable to speak. He stood before them for another moment. Then, he turned and walked into the house, leaving them outside.

Jesus sat down again and continued talking with the people. After a while, someone said to him: "Jesus, did you know your mother and brothers are still waiting for you?"

Jesus burst out: "Who is my mother? Who is my brother? Those who seek *metanoia* so that they may see the Kingdom of Heaven: these are my mother and brothers." And he gestured at his friends.

When the meeting was over, he spoke privately to Simon. "You are right, Simon," he said. "We can't sit here any longer. We'll travel out among the people and tell them the good news."

So they began to make preparations right away. Jesus appointed Judas treasurer and the Sicariot collected money from the group's supporters. Once again, Susannah gave generously of her dower so they would not go hungry on the road.

And when they were ready, they left Capernaum on a mission to all of Galilee. And they were: Jesus and Simon and Sarah, Andrew and his wife Deborah, James and John, Philip and Bartholomew, and Judas the wealthy, son of James, Mary the Magdalene, Levi the tax collector, Thomas, James, the son of Alphaeus, Simon the Zealot, and Judas Sicariot, who would betray them.

2. More of the Tale of Mary Magdalene.

Mary is in Simon's house, serving wine to a group of men, and she thinks: "What the fuck am I doing here? That's what I want to know, anyway. Lord, ain't it better to be a whore than a servant, let them slave and slather for your body than your body slave for them where they sit talking of high and mighty things not a one of them better than the dream he dreams of me. At night. When no one's looking and he's got it clutched in his calloused fist and wishing it was clutched in mine. Soft, these hands, or were, they won't be soon. I watch them. And I used to wear how many rings and some of them given to me by men with the money to buy and sell these fishermen. It's all right for Susannah maybe when she's old now and he respects her, Jesus, treats her like he would anyone asking her for advice but you can't go back, can you, and have a life like hers, all married and virtuous so they treat you that way so what's the use trying? So she says to me: 'This is what you do.' Not: 'Would you mind, please, Mary,' with her back straight and her face fine and her hair silver carrying herself like a queen cause her husband up and died and left her the fishing money. 'This is how you make the bread,' and what was I to do without a penny in my purse not that I couldn't. But a roof's a roof, anyway, and I wanted to see. And I watch these hands, try to see them, in the last dark, with the men out having their good time on the water, and I hoist the amphora in the dark, thought it'd crush me, and Susannah says, 'Carry it this way,' and she walks off with it on her head as if I've never seen a woman go for water—my mother's maids, I wanted to say . . . But I didn't. Couldn't let such an old one show me up, so off I go staggering under the damn thing out to the well like I'm the old one. And Sarah chattering like a biddy. Well, it's easy, when you're married, don't have to care how you act, anymore; gossiping. Water drawn deep red sparkle like a sigh to the soul these hands wore rings. For them. Toting them wine like a servant girl, why don't they get up and get it themselves. Jesus, at least, says thank you. Judas, he stares. I know what they're all thinking. Why the fuck did I come? I watch these soft, smooth, caress me never lonely hands the light on them warm and white as the sun breathes like God into the red morning all whitestreaked with flour and water little fists thumping and wrestling the dough into loaves and before the baking white hot sun the red warm glow of the oven on them shoveling in the ones that have risen and what makes her so pleased with herself Sarah puffing to blow the hair off her forehead, brushing it with fingers streaking her forehead white with the flour. Well, Simon doesn't treat her badly. I hear them in the night. Look at him, sitting cross-legged on the floor beside his Lord and master, Jesus, and gazing at him and he isn't even talking, for God's sake, just listening to that, whatever he is, smelly tanner, bitch and moan about the tax. Simon all sharp-eyed like he had his hooks in every word, almost bouncing, sitting there, like someone set his ass on fire no better than the dreams he has at night and I know his kind turning her over always going for the backside wants her faceless giving her, Sarah, the slap and tickle here and there while she blushes red bum cheeks red giggling till he bears down over her hammering at her grabbing her ass like the reins

of a chariot riding her and she likes it likes it the way I hear her
gasping and giggling in the dark and she can't see: that's what
he is. Is. The power he wants or not the power but the ride, the
making it go his way, sure. Sure, she kneels to give the wine to
him, blushes even when he deigns to thank her, and look at
that look they give each other: Last night. I'd know just what
to say to make him spill in a minute. Where to touch him.
With these hands. And they weren't half bad at the spinning
either. Even Susannah said so. Said I took to it: well, a little
nimbleness is all it takes, and the flax on your shoulder and the
heavy spindle twirling at your knees and the shade of the
courtyard tree from the late white morning all the grass dead
all the soil dust dry in your nostrils painting red cracks in your
hands and Sarah singing, Susannah doing the mending under
the wall and humming to herself, robe across her knee like a
child soft old wrinkled swift expert hands. These hands wore
rings and gutting fish in the afternoon. Waiting on the shore
for the men, coming in, laughing, Sarah waving wives brown
Judas with that monster muscled chest like the heroes in
stories how you picture them. Coming right to me. Best catch
in his boat, always in his boat now he's sober and looking at me
while he loads up my basket with them flopping around,
gasping, dying, funny they can't breathe air. Guts all colorful
yellow blue red but bright the only bright thing in the
colorless wash of that afternoon sun so your sweat drips into
them when you stop rubbing your sleeve over your brow to
yank their guts out and hurl them in the big jar for jelly and
the husk into the basket for meat and then another one, slit it
down the middle I can think of plenty I'd like to do that to and
open them on the yellow blue red how can anything be so blue
and yellow in them? And your hands running red and juicy red

97

and pale with their blood and juices streaking the dust. Why doesn't he talk to me anymore? Just staring sometimes catch him watching with his fierce brown eyes. Couldn't have him anyway not here with them all and not being married probably thinks he'd have to pay me well maybe he would. Leaning against the beam with his big shoulder, frowning down on Jesus, listening to every word he says, never talking, never touching his wine except to wet his lips which I notice have been nursing the same cup of it since the meeting began. And what's that rich-looking one want here anyway? Always the way: worried about his immortal soul now he's made his stash, saying: 'How can I achieve the Kingdom of Heaven?' Jesus has his number: 'Give away everything you own.' Right, sure he will. Even laughs, even says: 'How would I feed and clothe my family, Rabbi?' And now Jesus goes into his routine how can anyone understand him, saying: 'Think about the lilies of the field. They neither spin like women nor toil like men. But Solomon at the peak of his glory was never clothed like one of them.' And Judas watching him like that was so wise how would he like it if I didn't spin and toil and serve him his bloody wine for him like I should starve in a ditch before I open my legs for a little wherewithal. They don't want you making a living off it because then they're not in control, that's why. And Judas frowning down at him all evening but he'd have been less happy if I hadn't had to do what I did and him who can't talk to me now cause a whore's what he needs to be gentle to. Probably going to the house here for it, I'll bet, cause he thinks maybe a woman seals up down there if she's decent and does a day's work instead of slutting it, cause he wants to so bad probably wants to make her beg for it, eat it, swallow it, take it and scream for more while he thinks, 'See?

See? You're a whore under it, strutting so pretty, so clean,'
where if you say to him, 'Lay your money down, my good
man,' it's all stroking you and kissing each part of you like you
were a rosy virgin, coming into you like a prayer does sometimes on a sweet spring morning, practically praying on you
for that matter until how can you help coming he makes such a
fuss over the whole thing. Doesn't look so big, does he,
standing there, looking at Jesus with the rest. Doesn't look so
all alone and above them and powerful like he did. All of them
staring at Jesus. What's he why the fuck did I big deal anyway
. . . Though I will say. Those eyes. Those black, black eyes he
has when he listens to you, Jesus, and the smile he has when
he's talking like it's all a joke to him. I see him. I see him,
sometimes, when he comes out into the court and sits there
against the wall and stares at you. He's got to have something
on his mind so that I heard Sarah, when we were down by the
water the other day waiting for the boats, and she's nattering
with Philip's little sister and the girl's saying this and that
about him to let Sarah know she's got the eye for him, and
Sarah says, kind of thinking on it, 'You know, he's not above a
little flirtation now and then, but I wouldn't put your hopes on
him. I think he stays above it.' And I want to say: There ain't
no above it. He's got a prick, ain't he. I've seen him piss with
it. You can step out of the game, but even that's in the game,
the game goes on in your head and it's still what you are. Being
so sweet with everyone, watching us in the courtyard, maybe
he's just like Judas only the other way: thinks you can't fuck
and be a good man, too. Plenty like that. Like women. Rather
be with us out in the court than with the men. I've had them
like that. Rather be taking it than giving it and you never
know which of them it'll be when they come in the tavern.

Only later upstairs. Jesus with his eyes make you feel like when they buried my little brother, little Jacob, in the cave and I wondered what's inside there at the very end coming in limp till you roll him over and he bends his ass up at you whimpering give it to me, Mary, spread his cheeks soft till his rosebud asshole's winking at you wanting it like a woman wet your fingers with a little cuntjuice slip it in him while he cries out like his own mother looking down at him while he roils and bucks and cries as if I were up in the sky or as if I were the sky with the murky water everywhere below me roiling bucking roaring waves and the cries of the damned drowning in it reaching me where I'm all serene and blue with the clouds rolling over me and my own face, the face of the sky, wild in the face of the waters washing over, filling the lungs of the numberless damned till I'm all breathless and exhilarated and wild and glad at the faces stretching up toward me for air, their eyes rolling back in terror, gleaming pearly on the sea, then going under, fingers clawing for a grip in the flesh of the sky— my flesh—then they sink and disappear and the sky breathes in the air of the whole world with satisfaction. I'd be up there in the clouds on a golden throne. Colossal and naked, my skin all ivory with a pinkish glow and panting with desire. Then Jesus would rise before me enormous as the sea. Wash over me, all over me like the sea and I'd rise up on the swell, swell up between his legs, go up inside him, my whole body swelling and growing in him till it fills him and we're one body together stretching out over everything, reaching out to embrace everything, pulling it all into us, pulling it all into us with these hands. These hands."

3. The Collector's Journal continues.

Jesus and the others traveled throughout Galilee. They slept beside the road, or in the fields beneath the stars. They stopped in towns and villages and cities. They stayed in the homes of friends, or in the homes of the strangers who took them in. Everywhere they went, Jesus spoke to the people. In synagogues, and houses, and fields and by the sea, he addressed the wise men and the women, the shepherds and the prostitutes, the artisans and the outcasts.

And he said to them: "Blessed are the poor in spirit: Theirs is the Kingdom of Heaven. Blessed are those that mourn: They will be comforted. Blessed are the meek: They'll inherit the earth. Blessed are those who hunger and thirst after goodness: They will be filled. Blessed are the merciful: Mercy will come to them. Blessed are the pure in heart: They will see God. Blessed are the peacemakers: They are God's children.

"And when the majority of men hate you, and when they turn away from you and point their fingers at you and call you evil, that is the time to rejoice. It is at this moment as it has always been: Just so, they turned away from the prophets and reviled them.

"You can't serve two masters. You'll hate one of them, and love the other—or, at least, cling to one and despise the other. You can't serve God, and be worldly. That's why I tell you: Don't think about how you'll live, or what you'll eat or drink, or how you'll clothe yourself. Hasn't life got more value than meat, and flesh more value than clothing? Look. Look at the birds, who neither sow nor reap, nor gather what they've reaped into barns. Your heavenly father feeds them. He won't feed you, too? Consider the lilies of the field, how they grow. They don't toil or spin, but even Solomon at the height of his glory was not dressed like one of these. Won't your heavenly father clothe you, as well?

"Instead of food and clothing, seek the Kingdom of Heaven.

"It is within you. It has already come. Ask for it, and it will be given to you. Seek it and you shall find it. Knock on the door, and the door will open to you.

"It's easy: Simply make no judgments. If you see somthing and it offends you, pluck out your eye. If you lay your hand on something and it disgusts you, cut off your hand. If you see a speck in your neighbor's eye, take the speck from your own. Don't even resist evil. If someone strikes you on the right cheek, offer him the other one, too. If someone takes you to court and sues you and wins your coat, let him have your cloak as well. You've heard it said: Love your neighbor and hate your enemy. I tell you: Love your enemies. Bless those who curse you. Do good to those who hate you, and pray for those who abuse and persecute you. Then you will be like God is, then He will be your father. For He makes the sun rise on the evil and on the good, and He sends the rain on the just and the unjust alike.

"Make no judgment—or you will be judged. Because the judgment that you make is only a judgment of yourself. The measure you mete out you mete out to yourself again.

"It is easy to understand. But it is hard to do. Not everyone who says to me, 'Oh, yes, Master,' will know the Kingdom of Heaven. The tree is the fruit. What you do, you are. Therefore, act toward your neighbor as if he were yourself. That is the prophets. That is the law."

Few people were swayed by Jesus. He spoke forcefully and authoritatively, but when the crowds heard what he asked of them, they said: "Are these John's words? Did he send you out to preach? Are you his successor? By whose authority are you speaking?"

And after every sermon, Jesus sat in dark meditation. And he spoke to Simon and Judas.

And he asked them: "What are they saying about me?"

After a while, Simon organized Jesus' followers. He sent them ahead to tell people Jesus was coming, so there would be crowds when the preacher arrived. It didn't work. Jesus spoke and the people heard him, and they rejected him.

And Jesus was more despondent than ever. Over and over, he said to Simon: "What are they saying about me? What are they saying about me now?"

The mission was a failure. Simon could see the darkness gathering in Jesus' eyes.

One day, as the group was seated at a campfire by the side of the road, a man approached them riding a mule. He stopped near them and asked for James and John. The brothers went aside with the rider, and the three spoke together. Then, James and John returned to the campfire. John was crying.

"My brother and I have to return to Capernaum, Jesus," he said, "Zebedee is dead. Our father is dead."

The others stood and offered their condolences. But even as they were speaking, Jesus rose to his feet as well. His mouth was pulled down and his eyes were burning with the firelight.

He lost control. He shouted at them: "Why are you deserting me? Let the dead bury their dead. He who doesn't hate his father and mother—his children—his own life—will never be free enough to enter the Kingdom of Heaven."

The whole company fell silent at these words. Jesus continued to glare at them. Then, with a curse, he wheeled, and strode from them into the darkness.

The others sat by the fire, shaking their heads. No one spoke. Only their eyes met moment after moment. Finally, at a motion from Simon, they all looked up.

They saw a silhouette approaching. Suddenly, there was a breeze and the fire flared. Jesus stood before them with his arms outstretched, his face seeming to float and fade in the scarlet flamelight.

And he said: "Let us pray together, my brothers."

Now it's the custom of the Jews to stand before their family graves and cover themselves with ashes while they repeat the prayer for the dead over and over. But Jesus said: "Let us pray once and together. Do you think our heavenly Father, who knows what we need before we speak, needs to hear our prayers spoken again and again?"

He put his hands on the shoulders of the two mourning brothers. He began to speak the prayer for the dead. But he did not. He said his own prayer in a loud, taut voice that seemed to want to storm heaven by main force.

He said: "Papa! *Heavenly* Father! Your name be blessed! Your kingdom come to us: Your will be done on earth as it is in heaven! Give us the bread we need today. Forgive us the wrongs we've done as we forgive the wrongs that were done to us. Do not lead us into temptation, but guide us away from evil. Yours is the kingdom! Yours is the power! Yours is the glory forever! Amen."

And then he raised his hands to the sky. And he raised his head and looked at the stars.

But the others looked at him: at his face streaked with tears, at the desperate gaze with which he scanned the stars as he burned like a star himself in the trembling firelight. And they all knew, looking at him, that the end of the mission was near.

In fact, it came soon after. They were in Cana. They were staying in the home of a potter named Saul.

A messenger came to them. He said: "I've come from Bethabara. The people of John the Baptist send you a message. They say: Proclaim yourself. Are you the one who is to come, or must we wait for another?"

Jesus couldn't answer, at first. Even when people had demanded it of him, he had not pretended to be John's successor. Still, he felt his mission had been worthwhile. So he said: "Go back to Bethabara. Tell them what I do and say. Let them decide who I am."

When the messenger had gone, Simon leapt to his feet. "The bastards," he shouted. "Who are they to demand this of you?"

"They're afraid I'll shame them," Jesus said.

"Yes," said Simon. "By speaking the words of John instead of seeking the power and petty politics of the monastery."

Jesus shook his head sadly. He said: "I want no more of this, Simon. I want to return to Capernaum."

Simon and Judas—all the others—protested.

But Jesus said: "I want to return to Capernaum. We will end our mission. We will wait for the liberation of John."

105

4. More of The Book of Judas.

Now when the time had come for Jesus to depart from Magdala, Judas followed after him. For he said:

"Where is the voice of the mighty
when the wise man speaks for the Lord?
And where is his power when the Lord opposes him?
he loves a whore who gives herself to kingdoms;
he follows a slave who falls to force of arms.
But trembling with the strength of his desire,
he trembles with fear in the midst of great cities
lest the wise man whisper in the wilderness
and the Lord be heard."

And he traveled with Jesus throughout the province. And Jesus preached to the people, saying: "Do not judge or you will be judged. And do not resist evil, but if a man should strike you on the right cheek, turn the other to him also. And if you go the strait and narrow way that few men go, you will find the Kingdom of Heaven."

And Judas heard these words and felt joy at them. And he sought within himself for the change of heart that would allow him to see the Kingdom of Heaven.

Now, when Jesus had left Magdala, Mary had also followed after him. And Judas saw her made glad among the women, and work among them so that she was not a harlot anymore.

And his love for her grew. But she did not speak to him. And when he approached her, she turned her face away from him. And he feared she would have nothing to do with him because they had lain together when she was a whore.

And Judas waited, thinking to win her when he had achieved *metanoia*. And he said in his heart:

"She was the age who gave herself to power.
She is eternity who is wisdom's now.
She was the harlot of warriors.
Now she is the wife of the man of God."

And Judas attended to Jesus. And they went from town to town spreading the good news of the change of heart and the Kingdom of Heaven.

And they came to a certain village in the hills of northern Galilee, where the people were shepherds. And they entered the synagogue, which was rude and made of wood and wattle. And it smelled of sheep dung which was all about.

And Jesus preached to the shepherds who came to him. And they grew angry at his sayings, and they murmured against him. And they began to shout at him. And when the crowd had grown noisy, one of the shepherds threw a stick at Jesus. And others began to throw sticks at him, and also bits of the sheep dung that lay on the floor.

And Jesus continued speaking quietly. But Judas conferred with Simon, who was chief among the disciples, saying: "Now I fear for the rabbi, even for his life."

And Simon and Judas ran to the front and grabbed Jesus by either arm. And they carried him from the synagogue while the other disciples held back the mob.

And the shepherds chased Jesus and his people to the edge

of the village, shouting and hurling sticks and stones and handfuls of dung. And one man rushed forward with a stick to belabor Jesus. And Judas smote the man on the head such that the man said, "Woh!" and staggered about for days afterward muttering bits of song.

And when they were out of the village, they fell by the side of the road breathless. And Jesus was sad, and said: "The disciple cannot be greater than the master. If the blind leads the blind, both fall into a ditch."

And Judas said to him: "Rabbi, you yourself have said, 'Rejoice when men hate you, for so was it with the prophets of old.' And lo, it was no fun for them either."

And Jesus cried out in anguish, saying: "The truth is everywhere about them, but they are blind to it. They know that when the clouds come in from the west there will be rain—why can't they read the signs of the times?"

And Judas rubbed his knuckles and said: "Everyone talks about salvation, but no one does anything about it."

And Judas now redoubled his efforts to find the Kingdom of Heaven through *metanoia*. And his heart was filled with thoughts of it, and with thoughts of Mary. For he knew she would love him when he entered the Kingdom, as she would love a conqueror.

Now it happened one day that Judas was walking alone in a garden, pondering these things. And he smiled to himself, for he imagined himself with Mary in the Kingdom.

And just at that time, Mary was sitting beneath a bay tree nearby, mending some clothes. And as she sat, she sang to herself, saying:

"Angels above you with wings of white
shield you and love you all through the night.

109

All through the night, the angels gleam,
and dream the dream of what we seem.
Heavenly light, the golden beam,
will stream from wings of white."

Now, Judas was passing, and he heard Mary's song. And he said: "Truly, this sound is beautiful." And seeking to find the source, he looked on Mary beneath the tree. And his heart was filled with love. And straightway, he approached her, saying:

"Why have you run from me
who was once married to you by the night?
And where have you gone that you have forgotten me?"

And Mary was startled. And she stood up, and dropped her mending to the ground, saying, "Why did you come after me, Judas? I was so peaceful here."

And Judas answered her, saying: "Don't be afraid of me. I came into you when you were my harlot, I want to come into you when you are my wife. I feel I could come into you forever."

But she blushed and said to him: "Feel another way, Judas. My love is perfect now."

And Judas wondered at her words, and said: "Is my love corrupt?"

And she said: "I don't know. I don't love you. I love Jesus. For he is bringing the Kingdom."

And Judas recoiled from her as if she had struck him. And he walked off alone into the fields, brooding on what she had said.

5. The Tale of Mary Magdalene continues.

Mary sits near the top of the hill while Jesus speaks, and she thinks: "Judas, he came to me. Judas, he said, 'Mary, I've been thinking. Are we in a dream?' I was washing our clothes by the stream and I don't know why I quick covered myself with the wet robe like I was naked or something, held it up before my breasts like they were showing. And for a minute, I thought he knew. About the dreams. About what I see. I couldn't talk to anyone else and I thought. But he said, 'We were all played out, you and me, and he came,' and I said to him, 'Yes, it's all different now.' Because he comes to me in the dreams, Jesus, and sometimes I think he's kneeling down beside me while I sleep to whisper them into my ear, putting them into my ear to fill up my head and I thought that and looked away from Judas with my cheeks hot. 'I feel swept up in something, taken away,' Judas said, and he took my shoulders to make me look at him. His fingers pressing into my flesh soft deep, but when I looked up at him, he's so tall, his head was against the sun all blacked out by it and I couldn't see his face, just the glow on the curling tips of his hair and the spokes of light flashing out from behind it and slipping away again. 'Maybe there'd be a place,' he said, 'where we can go. Where there's no Rome or anything to fight with. We could be ordinary people then. With kids then maybe. I don't know. Whenever I'm around him, everything seems more important than it is.' And I said—still clutching the robe up to me and the damp of it

111

seeping through the robe clammy on my skin—I said, 'Then you're only pretending, pretending to believe in him.' And he let me go. He stepped back so the sun came out over him and made me squint and turn my head. 'Believe in him?' he said. 'What is he?' And I opened my mouth to say and couldn't express it because it's in the dreams that come to me every night in the tents or out beside the fire when we sleep under the stars when I see the light of heaven coming into us together and we're one, a single stroke of sunlightning pinning me where I am filling him so that I wake wet and panting and hungry to see him and when he stands up on the hill like this and speaks I feel myself my soul my self coming out of his mouth in his words and he must feel it too though he never says it to kneel by me in the night and whisper me my dreams. I hardly know what I'm thinking. I hardly know what I'm thinking. I don't know when it happened. When. One day, he came all new to me in Capernaum, or over the days—new like he is now up there on the hill saying, 'Judge not of right and wrong,' like he said, 'Throw the first stone if you've done no evil.' Standing up there in the bluing cool of afternoon the grass around his feet. I remember one day I was making the bread with Susannah. Pounding and pounding the dough into softness with her rolling the dough beside me. And I was looking at my hands white with flour, streaked with water, and I saw—I saw suddenly—the water was falling, falling onto my hands, running down into the web of my thumb and onto the backs and down my wrist streaking the white flour. And I looked around not knowing where I was, and Susannah she said to me, 'Not too much salt in the bread,' and I threw myself at her, crying while she held me on her breast, and all I know was that I was saying, 'I don't want to be a whore

anymore. I don't want to be a whore anymore,' over and over.
And I knew that it was all Jesus, too. It was like I'd been
thinking and thinking about it without knowing it. Thinking
about being a part of him and how he has to, he has to love you
when you are because you're his own self. And that's what he's
saying. That's what he's saying now about John. How we're
part of him, and he's part of John who is God, who is with God
because he's a prophet like in the scriptures only Jesus is just
Jesus who's right here. That's the Kingdom of Heaven. And I
started to dream about the bolt of sunlightning. About the sky
the way it is in summer clear of everything and the blue of it
almost white with the heat only not shimmering, not even
shimmering, it's so clear. And Jesus, talking, the way he is
now, standing there with his black eyes and his black hair
curling and the light from nowhere—cause there's no sun in
the dream—making a halo all around him, and I'm looking,
I'm looking for myself cause I can't see me, and suddenly I
realize that I'm inside him, that I went up into him and now
I'm inside. And when I realize that, out of the unshimmering
white-blue sky, the whole sun comes in one hot fiery bolt—all
the sun in it, that one flashing bolt—and pins me with God so
I see, I see the whole world's in Jesus and I am, too. So I said to
Judas, finally, 'I don't know. Don't you know? When he talks.
With his eyes. He has everything in him somehow.' And Judas
looked down at the rich dark soil of the stream bank and the
little shoots there edging their heads into the world so green
and he shook his head at his sandals and he said, 'Not everything.' And I wanted to tell him, I wanted him to know, I
said, 'I have dreams, Judas.' And he said, 'Yes, it's like a
dream.' And I could see how he didn't understand. And I
couldn't tell him. About the bread. About how I make the

bread for Jesus, and when I see his teeth tear into it my saliva flows, and I pour the wine into the cups from the big amphora tasting it bitter and rich on my tongue because he will drink it. And I don't want to be a whore anymore. I should listen to him, to Jesus, now. I shouldn't let Judas take me away, thinking of Judas how he stands and frowns up at him from beside me on the hill and I know he's not really believing, false, false, false. I should think about Jesus' words that are me coming out of him saying my soul that he knows. But Judas, he touched my cheek. Judas, he turned away sad, I would save him but he will be in the sea when the big sea roils under the sky we are together and they drown, the damned, in it, Judas because he wants to have me back to what I was so he can come inside me instead of the orange fire bolt of sunlightning out of the unshimmering sky and take up the only place where God can come to both of us, Jesus and me. I have to train my eyes, my heart, on Jesus where he speaks above me, the outline of him black against the sky as if he's floating there in it. And Judas walked away. When I was standing by the river, Judas looked down at me once sadly and full of remembering I could tell about that time so that for a moment I felt the warm hard and soft filling flash and my cheeks flushed and the damp of the stream water seeping through to my chest soured with sweat. Then he turned and walked away, his head down and I wanted to lean over him where he was drowning in the wild sea of damnation and offer him the rosy tit of the sky and let him suck the life of it. But if I called to him. But if I followed after. Little breaths, taking little breaths. Listen to Jesus and stare up at him where he is speaking me into the hearts. Into the hearts of the people on the hill. They still don't listen. They

still don't believe. Drown, drown, drown in the sea, they will,
Jesus. We are the sky together, Jesus, up above the hill our
arms spread to be. Waiting for the sweet, warm, hard, soft
sunbolt. Yes, yes. I didn't. I didn't follow Judas. Let him go
up over the little hill to the camp. Didn't. Listen. Listen. To
Jesus. I follow you, Jesus. I follow you."

6. The Collector's Journal, containing the sixth poem in the Jesus cycle.

Jesus returned to Capernaum by a circuitous route, preaching the word of John as he went.

After several weeks, he and his followers came within sight of the sails upon Lake Gennesaret, and the little group rejoiced together to see their homes again.

They had not been home long, however, when disaster struck.

Jesus and his friends were down by the lakeside, working on their fishing equipment. There was a crowd around them, asking them questions about their journey and conversing with them on deeper matters as they used to do. Jesus was kneeling on board a beached boat, knocking a plank into place with a hammer. All at once, his hand paused in midair. His face came up and he stared into the crowd. He stood, stepped down onto the sand, pushed past the others until he came before a woman. She was a beautiful woman with long, fair hair tumbling out about her fine features from the cowl she wore. She and Jesus stared at one another for a long time while the crowd fell silent around them.

Then the woman said: "You are Jesus of Nazareth."

"Yes," said Jesus. "And you are Joanna."

Because the woman was the wife of Antipas' steward Chuza: She was the disciple of John who had come to warn the Baptist before the fortress at Machaerus.

117

Now, she began to cry, and seeing this, Jesus trembled from head to foot.

"Tell me," he said.

But Joanna could not speak.

"Tell me!" Jesus cried out to her.

Joanna sank to her knees. She raised her fists to her eyes in a seizure of sobbing.

Jesus lifted his face to heaven and wailed as if the soul were being torn out of him. Because he knew that John the Baptist was dead.

This is the sixth verse in the cycle:

She must have danced.
She must have: turned
and spun and pranced
till Herod burned
for her. She'd heard
John's voice, God's word,
Hell's curse: 'Incest!'
It pierced her breast.
'Silence the man!'
she must have said,
'Silence the man!
Bring me his head.'
Herod delayed.
And so she swayed
for him; eased down
her silken gown;
bent back her hips
until he saw

118

her underlips
all red and raw
and wet. While John
preached on and on,
Herod, enthroned,
looked on and moaned.
Then, his jaw fell.
He saw her cunt
ripple and swell
till, with a grunt,
out pushed a head,
its eyes blood red,
its jagged grin
and bearded chin
writhing. The rest
soon followed, too:
Shoulders and chest
came struggling through;
loins, legs and feet . . .
A man—complete—
was born. He roared
and drew a sword.
And she then purred:
'Just say the word.'
And Herod did.
She knelt. She laughed.
Her slick lips slid
down Herod's shaft,
to suck and lick
the stiffened prick.

119

Son of Man

While Herod gasped,
the swordsman grasped
the Baptist's hair;
he raised his blade
high in the air,
and slowly made
John lift his chin.
The sword went in.
John's throat spewed out
a crimson gout.
And she? She sucked
the ruler's rod
till Herod bucked
and shot his wad.
Then Herod stood.
He whispered, 'Good.'
He gave John's head
to her, and said:
'Now head for head.
And should one rise
up from the dead
again, he dies
this very death.'
And, out of breath,
he sat, and signed
for food—and dined.

PART IV: THE TRANSFIGURATION

1. The Collector's Journal continues.

Jesus broke down. The news of the Baptist's death felled him like a blow. He retired to Simon's house in mourning, spoke to no one, did nothing. All his work, his discourses—everything was suspended; and even simple actions like eating and conversation seemed to have lost all interest for him. During the day, he sat motionless in the courtyard, watching the women work, or he walked by the sea alone. At night, he called out in his sleep in a voice that filled everyone who heard it with embarrassment and terror.

Simon grew worried, not only about his friend, but also the situation in the town. He said to Jesus:

"Unless I'm mistaken, this is a dangerous time. Herod has been said to ask about you: to wonder aloud if you are a newly risen John. He'll be watching us to see if we try to revive the mission, and the Herodians and Pharisees won't fail to act, knowing they have such an ally. I think we should get out of here. We should go into neighboring Perea, where Philip rules wisely and leniently. We won't be persecuted there."

Jesus, disconsolate, allowed himself to be guided by his friend.

So the group left Capernaum again. They traveled into Perea. Simon's plan was to remain in the fishing towns near the sea where friends and colleagues would sustain them. But now Jesus spoke for himself.

"I want to withdraw into a lonely place," he said.

The others could say nothing to dissuade him. They followed him inland.

They journeyed into the mountains that rise purple and gray against the sky. Finally, they came to a stark valley at a mountain's base.

"I am going up into the mountain to fast and pray," Jesus said.

And slowly, he wended his way up a steep goatpath, entered the rings of mist that circled the mountain's peak, and vanished from sight.

Those who were with him camped in the valley, near a stream. They waited for a day, but Jesus did not return. They waited for another day with the peaks looming over them. Still, there was no sign of Jesus. They talked among themselves.

John said to James: "You know how it is at dawn on the water? When the birds start singing, just at dawn, when it's real quiet, just before the wind rises and the sails begin snapping? I always hurled my net just then. Like this. Watch: This was my method. It made my muscles ripple. There was a girl named Naomi who used to come down to the strand early to watch."

And James said: "When John was alive, we knew the Lord was with us."

And others of them began to talk in the same way.

Simon heard them. On the second evening, when they sat around the fire, he laughed and said to them:

"I feel like we're the children of Israel, waiting for Moses at the bottom of the mountain. Shall we build a golden calf?"

His joke made them ashamed, and they were quiet for yet another day, waiting for Jesus.

2. More of the Tale of Mary Magdalene.

Jesus is fasting on a mountaintop in a lonely country. In the night, Mary rises from the camp and walks down a path. It is lined with a tangle of thorny branches, winter bare. She comes into a bower: a circle almost enclosed by indigo stone. Above is a roof of interlacing branches. The stars and the full moon shine through. She kneels, the hem of her white robe spread in the dust around her. And she thinks: "Oh God, and when he heard. And when she told him, and when he heard, his eyes— he opened them so wide that I could never stop seeing. It was like falling into them. It was like when they found baby brother, little Jacob, drowned in the little wading pond, tangled in the weeds as if they'd wrapped themselves around him for love and held him there until he agreed to stay. And I thought: Naughty Jacob, he was playing with himself. Because he liked to see his reflection on the water and mother said, 'Not too close.' But he liked to reach for it and sometimes cried when he splashed it and it disappeared. And I thought: That's what happened. He decided to dive in and see where he was in there. When they found him there was no reflection anymore because Jacob had gone through it down to the bottom and he drowned. With God. Mommy said. Who wrapped his loving arms around him while he struggled to come back up to where his laughing image played on the little ripples. Oh. Oh. Oh. Oh, when Jesus opened up his eyes. Is the moon a good sign? Or is it bad? Does it mean he'll live or

125

die? You have to know how to interpret these things. What am I. I wanted. But he knew I was bad. I wanted to comfort him as he had come to me and given me my dream. I wanted to. When he sat, his eyes wide and I couldn't stop seeing, against the courtyard wall and I wanted to come to him and put his head against my breast until his lips grew around the pink nipple and his body formed into the cradle of my arms and I was all big white and rosy and he crawled over the ivory plain of my belly and nuzzled with his nose between my legs and I would gently press his bottom with a finger till he slid up into me. I wanted to comfort him. I had washed his feet before. Sometimes when he sat with the others, I had knelt at his feet and poured the oil on them and rubbed it with my hair till he said, 'Thank you, Mary,' and I was glad because he knew we were together. I wanted them to see, all of them. I wanted them all to see me kneeling at his feet, it made me feel so warm to kneel there. But I was bad all the time. I had gone into him. I had gone into him and I thought . . . But no, I was only growing into the union of my aborted womb and every wine-dribbling fish-reeking callus-fingered fisherman who ever spurt his seed into my every hole. Oh God. Oh God, I pray, don't. Send. Send me the moonsign is it good or bad. Don't kill him for my sin, all that sin, piling it up into the scale of life and death, then send your sunbolt into me, up my ass, spill your Godseed into the shit of me until they grow together and they reach into me and pull out the weed-en-twisted body of his dying and I'll die. I only wanted to comfort him. When he sat in the courtyard. After he'd heard. That John was dead who was the bringer of God into his union with me reach out of the shadow of his death his staff into my asshole and I stood from beneath the tree where Susannah who

126

had held me like a mother in her arms on my returning she and I were spinning the wool together and I stood and saw from the corner of my eye her hand reach up restraining and her lips parted on the word she never spoke to stop me and I walked across the heat dry courtyard dust my bare feet burning and I knelt beside him where he sat his eyes wide, staring into the heat. And I was crying. And my tears rolled clean I thought pure over my cheeks and fell and fell on his feet and made little dark brown stains on the sandal straps while he sat staring and I knelt down and washed his feet with my hair and my tears. Oh God, oh God, don't kill him for my sin. My thousand thousand sins. My throat swallowing scum and my belly shat on by a man who paid me extra and my ass ripped open by hot tongues and Judas in me forcing me to love it gentle, forcing me but I sinned and woke to him touching me everywhere and loved it and adored him and only followed Jesus to have it happen again and that's why when he felt my soft hair on his feet cleaning my clean tears and he swam up out of the death at the bottom of his eyes so empty his body it seemed could hardly keep its shape with so much nothing at the center. And he swam up out of his eyes no wonder and looked down at me where I was kneeling and his voice came from out of the back dark of the cave where they buried him and said, 'Get away.' I raised my tears into the glitter of the sun but he was in the shadow of the wall I raised my face. And he said, 'Get away from me. Get her away, damn it.' And I could see he was thinking: Whores! And then Susannah had me, 'Leave him alone,' by the shoulders, pulling me away . . . Night. I'm cold. With the full moon sinking. And a lighter violet rising into the darkness of the sky. The branches black and silver and tangled over me. The sun will come suddenly. It's a sign of

good luck the moon. Or bad luck maybe. The sun will come
and I will die and I will send, maybe I can send the best of my
soul up the mountain to him and fill him as he must be full of
light, growing bigger as the light within him grows until he is
the light and everywhere and I am gone. Oh God. Will strike
him down for my pride. For my pride and sin in trying to. But
if I could maybe the sun. Oh God, it's happening, my fault,
my fault I couldn't be him, something, the sky. Is growing
violet and the moon is almost gone. It was a sign of good I can
see and it's sinking away for my pride which I. Oh God,
someone is coming. Someone is coming to me now down the
path and the sun will break with a single bolt over the rocks
and kill me it is coming now and he is Jesus with John to do it
for my sin I wasn't Jacob I don't know what I'm what I'm Jesus
and John together who is that who is that footsteps on the path
I don't oh come to me come to me take me into the living life
of death for all my sin I can't he's coming faster faster down the
path I love the eternal I love the eternal I love the eternal. The
sun. A bolt of first sunlightning over the purple rocks to strike
me white the red blood in me rising to it oh oh oh the who
who is it who is it on the path the sun I see. Judas. Oh, Judas.
Oh, thank God, thank God."

3. The Book of Judas continues.

Now, soon after this time, a messenger came to Jesus and said: "John the Baptist is dead." For Herod Antipas had finally had him executed. And when Jesus heard this, he cried out in a loud voice. And he departed across Gennesaret to a deserted place, and he climbed to the top of a mountain to fast and pray. And Judas waited below with Simon and the other disciples.

And Judas began to doubt Jesus in his heart. And he said:

"Were there no graves in my own soul
that I am buried in his desires?
Had I no kingdom of my own flesh
that I live and die with him?"

And he thought of the days in Magdala, when he had drunk wine. And he remembered how he had lain with Mary. And he laid eyes on Mary, who was also waiting beneath the mountain. And he said: "I have become a dream apart from myself." And he desired her.

Now, Simon saw that the disciples were murmuring against Jesus. And he said to them: "I will go up into the mountain and speak to him that you will believe in his return."

And Simon climbed up the mountain that day and was upon the mountain with Jesus many hours. And when darkness had fallen, the disciples saw Simon descending. And when he reached them, they saw that his face was wild; and it was covered with dust and streaked with tears. And he would not speak to them, but withdrew apart.

And the disciples were fearful and said to each other: "Is Jesus dead?" But Simon would not speak to them.

And the disciples slept. But when it was almost dawn, Judas rose in secret and went in search of Simon.

And Judas found the disciple standing on a rock above the valley, and looking into the distance. And when Simon saw Judas approach, he turned to him, and Judas saw his face was weary.

And Simon said, "What am I, then, that I have followed him?"

And Judas knew that Jesus had gone mad.

And Judas felt a great joy well up in him such that he was afraid of himself. And he ran through the camp searching for Mary, saying:

"Let me be free, sweet Heaven.
Let me hold her in my hands.
My body runs before me,
remembering desire."

And Judas ran down a path into a bower. And he came upon Mary there, praying on her knees. And he was afraid and did not approach her.

And Mary heard his footstep. And straightway, she rose from the dust and came to him. And she was in an ecstasy.

And Judas took her into his arms and pulled her to the ground. And he came into her and they cried out to each other:

"I was one wandering:
forests and phantoms,
dreaming and waking.
I was alone.

Come to me, come to me, love.
Bring yourself to me.
I am easy and open to you,
and gentle everywhere.

I have been journeying,
through moonlight nations.
I, who imagined the moon.
My life is empty.

Bring yourself to me, love.
Pleasure is the world beyond you.
Even your thousand imaginations,
I will become.

Vinelands and jungles:
I struggled through them.
I looked behind me
at an empty plain.

Come to me, come to me, love.
Divide me and become my center.
I will make you endless for a moment.
I am not afraid of you.

Son of Man

Your lips, your loins, the melting of your loins,
your kiss, the coming into you.
Your hips, your breasts, your crying out around me,
the being inside you, the being where you are.

Bring yourself to me, love.
What the light enters, the light becomes.
What is entered by the light, becomes the light.
Whatever loves is certain of eternity."

And Judas and Mary lay naked in each other's arms for a long time. And when the sun was high above the mountains, there came a great cry from the camp. And Judas and Mary looked at each other and were afraid.

And when the cry came again, Mary leapt to her feet and shouted out to heaven. And Judas begged her to stay with him and not to heed the cry. But the cry came yet again from the camp.

And Mary put her fingers to her lips and her eyes filled with tears. And she said: "God forgive me!" And she ran to the camp.

And Judas rose from his bed of earth and followed her.

And when they came to the camp, they found Simon and the others standing beneath the mountain. And their faces were lifted to the peak.

And Judas and Mary likewise lifted up their eyes. And they saw a thin mist covering the peak. And in the mist, there was a shadow. And the shadow became a figure. And the figure stepped out before them.

And it was Jesus, moving down through the mist like a wraith.

And Mary let out a cry and fell to her knees. And Judas stood staring and amazed. For Jesus' face was transfigured before them: And it was full of light.

And Judas did not know whether to mourn or to rejoice. For he saw that Mary had fallen to her knees before Jesus, and he knew that he had lost her.

But he saw Jesus also, and he knew that Jesus had entered the Kingdom.

4. The Collector's Journal, containing the seventh poem
in the Jesus cycle.

Soon, Simon saw that the people would wait no longer, and
he decided he had to go up the mountain and speak with Jesus
himself. He climbed up the path until he came to a precipice of
stone just beneath the mountain's peak. There was Jesus,
seated at the very edge. The Nazarene's face was haggard, and
his eyes were lit as if fires burned behind them. Simon was
afraid for him.

"Jesus," he said gently.

When Jesus heard Simon speak, he turned to him with a
smile that made the disciple's blood run cold. He began
speaking quietly, but soon his voice had risen and he was
raving.

"Nobody knows who I am," he said. "I'm in a dungeon,
watching. If I call out, she will take me to the altar place
where he will cut off my head. Oh, Simon, there are flies up
here. Whenever I come near a moment of peace, they're all over
me. The flies. Oh God, they'll make me mad. It's a sign:
They're saying she won't kill me if I'll be silent. But what will
I do with my visions? When will I be light, be bodiless light
flowing into her virginity where she bends obedient in my
physical form to receive me? When will I bear my Lord the
light? Be mother of the light? I will be born the light. Damn
them, damn them . . . God, God, God. I will announce me
from Heaven as the son of the Lord, and then descend in wrath

135

and glory. First, the rich will burn a thousand days, and I will tear down the temple of the Sadducees, then the people will come to me for wisdom, and the poor and the oppressed will rise and follow me, their women bending before me, their men eunuchs in service of the Kingdom. God, God, God, they are making me mad . . . Come into me now, light, come into me."

And with that, Jesus leapt to his feet, still raving in a hoarse and cracking voice, and sobbing now so that Simon thought it would shiver him to pieces. Simon put his arms around his friend, and Jesus wept piteously, alternately pleading for the light, and railing at the mighty whom he threatened to destroy. Simon could hardly bear it. He was terrified, thinking Jesus would do him harm; and his heart was breaking, watching his friend's collapse.

At last, he pulled away. Jesus cried out: "Don't leave me." But then he screamed: "You are trying to hurt me. You are. You are."

Weeping himself now, Simon turned from him and started down the mountain. He hurried, stumbling along the goat-path until he reached the bottom. There, the disciples surrounded him, clamoring for news of Jesus. For once, Simon could not think what to tell them. He pushed them aside and went off by himself.

By this time, it had grown dark. The full moon had risen to the zenith, and was now beginning to go down. Simon climbed onto a boulder and sat staring into the valley. Just as the moon began to sink behind the mountains, and the eastern sky began to lighten with the coming of the sun, Judas Sicariot approached him.

Judas studied his face. "Why did we follow him?" he asked at last.

"Because our lives were miserable," said Simon.

And Judas asked: "Is Caesar miserable?"

"Yes," Simon said. Then: "I don't know."

Judas began to walk away. But he paused. He glanced up at the misty mountain on which Jesus sat. "I'm almost afraid, Simon," he said. "There's something in him that seems to thrive when he's broken. Resurrection is the nature of the man. I'm certain of it."

But Simon answered bitterly: "He is finished."

Judas left him, and Simon sat alone while the sun rose. Finally, his wife, Sarah, came to him, and stood beside him.

"You didn't come to bed last night," she said.

Simon's lips trembled. "I have no children," he said. And then he laid his head upon her breast and wept.

In another moment, there came a tremendous shout from the camp. Simon heard the others calling his name and Jesus' name. He took his wife by the hand and ran back to them. He found the others standing beneath the mountain, pointing upward. Jesus was descending.

Simon looked on, afraid. For a long time, only a vague figure could be seen wavering on the screen of the mountain mist. Slowly, that figure resolved itself into the silhouette of a man. Then, suddenly, the shadow flared out as if it had become a giant bird and were taking flight, and at the same instant, Jesus stepped through the mist and into the clear air.

Simon was stunned. Jesus' face was completely transfigured. All trace of madness was gone, and in its place was a serenity that Simon had not seen even in the infinite eyes of the Baptist

137

himself. The others saw it too and stood thunderstruck. Some of them wept openly; and Mary Magdalene fell to her knees before the man.

Jesus continued to descend until he reached the base of the mountain. Now, Simon rushed to him.

"Master," he said.

Jesus smiled and laid a hand on his shoulder.

Simon could barely speak. "We'll . . . we'll build a monument," he stammered. "We'll put up a rock as an altar here so men will know, and they'll come and they'll build a temple in your name and . . ."

Jesus laughed. "Stop talking like an idiot," he said. "There'll be no rocks or altars or temples in my name. You are the rock on which I will build my temple. Your understanding." Then, he looked around at all of them, and he said: "As for me, I am going to Jerusalem."

No one answered him. They were shocked and afraid.

Finally, Simon spoke for them all. "But you know the time is wrong," he said. "You'll be arrested. You could be killed."

But Jesus, still smiling, turned his back on Simon for all to see. And again he said: "I am going to Jerusalem."

And then and there, they all agreed they would go with him, even if it meant dying. Because they looked upon his face and they knew: Sometime, up on the mountain, he had heard what Elijah heard, and seen what Moses saw. He had entered the Kingdom.

This, the seventh poem in the collection, recounts the vision Jesus had had:

A lark upon the summit of a stone
sang suddenly and suddenly I woke.

The full moon to my right
slid down the sky, while to my left,
from overlapping peaks,
the sun rose, and look:
the precipice, its chance designs
bubbling to the surface of the dimming shadows:
the black pass slashed by the fallen tree;
the ridge of standing rock;
the white pinnacle, and the grey hoist
of the far hills with their handfuls,
here and there, of silver sea—
all of them burned, ah burned into their naked presence
under the pale sky; the birdsong.

I closed my eyes (the sun).
And drew a breath (the lark).
Traced it unfurling over
the landscape of a sad season,
while like a whisper it skit
along the branches and the roots
until it mingled with the swamp hiss
and the broken shoots,
and the thickening gas
of rosy carnage on the grass
swallowed it.
Starless, I think, this breath: a cry:
I am the sudden man who sees!
I see a man: the sudden man who sees:
a prophet of uncanny grace
abrupt as a spout of flame;
a whole generation with its abdomen clenched,

Son of Man

and its arched hands lit with the desire
to be buried in his red back;
its lips parched and its throat convulsing
to be nourished by his seed.
Oh, if we could cower in his shadow from the heat—
larksong, leafwind, locust burr—
or read his lineage on the empty page
or inhale his beasts
and have them swirl across our bellies like
larksong. Leafwind. Locust burr . . .
A drought upon your mutant fertility!
Better no gardens grow than your gardens!
Better to starve than to dine
on the fruit of withheld defiance!
Yes, well. The fact is I am left with this:
I hate them.
They have sent these frenzied ants into the earth:
dancers at blood pots worshipping a stone
for the bringing of rain.
And there: the fallen tree; the scarred, white rock:
the hobbled king, and Jezebel: her smile:
a gash sliced with a fingernail on the temple's wall.
When will my bowels stop gurgling
with the watery uncoiling of her hand
as she looses a swarm of false priests and lingams
on the high places of Israel?
I flatten with the expelled breath
like Astarte under the weight of her lover
and expanding, send him forth, my son,
on the leash of my envy:

His perennial daughter, I will make of him
my perennial child . . .
A drought, a drought upon this country!
I see Ahab, the king, and Queen Jezebel's shadows
fall like men into a pit
upon the nation opposite:
that river in the crystal hills;
that canopy of mist on distant trees.
The very breath of the mountain air is filled with the lark's music.

Sensation meditates upon sensation:
a river weaving through the hills—
the ancient hills, the crystal hills.
The banks are green with leaves and grasses,
and yellow where they have been dashed by the sun.
Naked at the waterside, the exile lies,
raised up on one hand braced against the ground.
The other arm hangs down across his waist
as, with his legs curled back into the grass,
his penis and testicles hang down one thigh
with patriarchal gravity.
Grave lips; grave eyes that gaze
through his undulate reflection
at the shades of minnows passing over stones.
Ravens bring him meat and bread,
urgently journeying above the dying country
until the river sighs away into the white sky;
until its surface breaks in ripples
on the pebbles of its bed;
until the rocks lie still and steaming

141

Son of Man

as a pavement in the sun.
Then, the ravens circle overhead;
the exile rises, travels on.
He stays with a widow and her infant son a while.
An esoteric haunt of humble rooms,
from room to humble room he palely passes:
Where she has lit the lantern in the niche,
and set dough on the windowsill to rise,
where she has taught her son to speak her name,
he passes. He walks the yard from wall to wall,
examining her spindle in his hand,
and when she turns, she finds him at the window.
Sometimes, he stands on the roof and surveys
the drought-wracked city,
his fist clenched, his features set,
desolate and unbending.
All well and good—
but sometimes, when she sits, the woman,
at twilight in cradle meditation,
and she reaches from her low stool,
and draws the steady creak of the rockers out of the dark—
well, desperately serene, she is.
She eats enough now, anyway,
but he won't touch her,
him and his wild eyes.
Every night, she goes to bed,
the meal jar's empty;
every morning, she wakes up,
it's full again;
the man's a magician,
but what's he do for fun?

Her child died once—of the hunger—
he carries him up to the roof—
he shouts at God: What rage is righteous, Father,
he says, that strikes down a child? he says.
She, for one, dove behind the oven,
waiting for the lightning bolt—
but no—there's a cough—
then three more quick ones,
like someone knocking at the door,
and she hears her baby, crying, alive . . .
What, precisely, if it isn't too bold to ask,
she would like to say,
is going on around here?
Grand things no doubt,
but sometimes, when she notices him
hovering round the cradle in the night,
she expects to see the moonlight fade,
and him with it—back where he belongs—
to fairyland.

Something of her voice, I think,
is like that gull's: wrenching, windward.
But something of it hankering, too,
like the whisper of the living leaves
fluttering after the clouds from their stems;
or just defiantly mortal, maybe,
like the rattle of dying leaves
whirling in the air around a cloud's procession,
and the patter of the leaves that fall
into the whir of hoppers in the sighing grass
where it chafes against the trunks of trees

while, overhead, a bird in the creaking branches
whistles three notes to a bird
and suddenly the locusts—
all discordant—how harmonious it sounds—
what an accidental music in a breath, a dream;
a memory, a breath, and visions;
a breath, the humming of a dream,
the sough of memory, a breath,
visions like songs
of the blood that runs in rivulets of the new rain:
An uncommon cinnabar, I'd say, where it burbles in those viscid
    pools,
a sweet carnation rose there,
where it weaves and rushes among the dead.

Elijah is triumphant over the priests of Baal.
His god and not their god has brought the rain.
He stands on a mound, the lingam behind him
toppled and shattered by the wind of the storm.
Bodies, in flashes of lightning, startle like thunder,
with the mad angles of their splintered limbs.
They cover the slope: the dead; the dead,
with eyes like brown glass,
peering into the reflectionless water.
Elijah is triumphant over the priests of Baal.
His arms uplifted and his teeth bared,
he orders them destroyed.
Quietly, a scepter in a half-severed hand,
tips over, falls and bobs away
on scarlet cataracts down the hill.
Mud is thinned and spattered and cleared

by the torrents and torrents of rain,
and a wound washed to the color of a peach.
The Israelites are hypnotized by the arcs of their own swords,
and they cannot stop:
Rhythmically, they are butchering the corpses.
Elijah is triumphant over the priests of Baal.

So this is the taste of tears—the salt sea.
And these must be the boundaries of flesh
which rise and fall to heaven and the earth;
these are the ears of the wind,
and the eyes of substance and light in relation;
these are the lips of what we do not know;
the opposing pinch of nipples;
and the breaths of the belly inventing the soul;
here the penis sways above
the impish, melancholy sac,
above the gravel of my thighs upon the gravel—
and, heavens, there am I:
keeping house in a tender anus,
ripe in its crevice
with the stench of productions
once tasted on the tongue like tears.
The poor wretch. In the aftermath,
with the mist lying over the carnage like a sheet:
There he sits on the hill, chin to knee,
hands to brow, blood to drink, flesh to eat.
Approaching slowly, oh, step by step by step:
A waver in the fog; a form;
regal among the carrion—
so he calls out to it: Ahab?

145

Son of Man

The mist shifts, disclosing her—
Oh no, it's that mad cunt again.
Elijah lifts his head, and softly—
louder—louder—keens . . .
until Jezebel slaps it down with a cry of her own.
Her voice is a knotted hawser,
drawing her to him step, oh, step by step,
and she's alive at every inch with murder.
"May the gods wreak upon me," she cries,
"what you have wreaked upon the manhood of Baal
if by tomorrow at this time
I have not done the same and more to you!"

Oh, Lord, Lord, Lord.
Really, I am no better than my father.
Just let me die.

Well, well: The uncaring sand within my chest
beats pulse on pulse the wilderness
where Elijah lies in the moonstruck sand,
and gestures of the night air
sprinkle the wastage of landscaping
over his body
as if to smooth him into the dunes.

Lord, let me die, I cannot stand
to gaze through this prism of decay
at the flame of eternity.

But even now, I open my eyes on the desert.

I see, as Adam saw, one like a woman
rising from my side.
Oh, she is radiant and transparent as a haze.
Dust blows through her on a breeze
and catches the starlight—look:
She fashions concentrated presence out of penetrated space
and the bow of her calves and the surge of her thighs,
her vagina's petals and whorls,
her belly, her breasts—that human face—
pour over me like honey
and I drink and drink her.

Oh, lay me as I were a child
within the mountain of the law,
soft in the crevice at its base,
bedded by scarlet wildflowers;
guarded and warmed by the entrance scrub,
enclosed in that frowning pillar of unspangled stone
which lours against the sky
as the sky circulates into starlessness
and the pale blue day.

Look! Look!
Elijah wakes, and he stands at the mouth of the cave
at the base of the mountain in the breaking morning,
and his eyes sweep over the wilderness, searching for the Lord.
And the sand curls in the fingers of a wind,
and then all that is green bows down;
rocks tumble from the mountain wall and shatter,
and the wind is gone and it was only the wind,

Son of Man

for the Lord was not in the wind.
And the earth quakes, and her breast is torn,
and all that was permanent falls to the ground,
and the mud-beasts scrabble from their holes and scatter,
and the quake subsides, and it was only a quake,
for the Lord was not in the earthquake.
And the dry brush crackles, ignites and flames,
and everything living is scorched and brown,
consumed in the raging red face of matter,
which settles to ash, and was only fire,
for the Lord was not in the fire.
And Elijah, peeling the holy from the substance of the elements,
and peeling the terrible from the substance of the elements,
hears, at last, the little voice of silence.
Listen: Larks have sung in our mornings:
Here, in a world where all illusion is illusion,
Moses stands before the burning bush
and peers into the flames.
Babies who cannot understand the word death
are burning in torment there—and die;
mothers with the terror of their necessity still in their breasts,
are consumed like paper,
and the muscles of men about to perform wonders
are made ashes instead;
soldiers hack themselves to pieces
in the navel of a rich man,
and the rich man dines on dung and then he burns;
psalm-singing famines and prayer-riddled plagues
hurl armfuls of broken innocents onto the flame
while survivors bow down to the smoke and murmur,
if they had not lived in the land of the famine . . .

if they had not dwelled in the country of the plague . . .
before a heartbeat chucks them in after
while the poet laughs, and under the poet's laughter
laughs the soundless dissolution of a stone
in the silence of the fire as it's burning unrelenting
on the silence of the bush as it is growing unconsumed,
and its branches spring like fountains
of semen, leukoreagh, sweat, tears, urine, excrement and blood
sprouting babies singing the hilarity of flesh everywhere
as vision, density and light become a flower
under its sun, the white-yellow sun,
on its grass, the yellow-green grass,
by its sea, the green-blue sea,
beneath its sky, the blue-white sky,
where the bush still blooms in moments
of revelation, orgasm and fear;
moments of stone, moments of branches,
an apple resting its shoulder on a ewer,
peacocks screeching, a beetle scratching over a leaf,
moments of moments
that still burgeon unconsumed in the silence of the fire
as it burns unquenched on the silence of the bush
in the silence of the eyes of Moses as he sees,
as he sees and, in his mortal pity,
cries out: Be thou thy name!
and hears, in answer, as the vision dies:
I AM.

I am,
on the other hand,
on this stupid mountain,

Son of Man

on this lovely morning—
no, it's almost noon.
The sun has risen high above the hills,
and I will mourn for John a little lifetime.
But, ah, well, well: I will go down.
Ah, yes, well, on waves of mortal pity,
I'll go down into the pleasant meadows of Israel
and her white-stoned towns.
I shall have to speak in parables and build a church of souls,
and I'll be welcome as boils everywhere, I imagine.
They shall see me and shout: Come,
let us break bread together
across the bridge of his nose . . .
I will go down where the moral squat
in the darkened corners,
fashioning clocks of their excrement
with its undigested bits of children's bones.
I will go down, and shall their yellow eyes
roll upward to behold me?
One or two or ten, perhaps,
shall toss all they've imagined in a sack,
heave the stuff to Gennesaret,
and follow me into themselves.
The rest, I trust, will devise for me—what sufferings?
I am not curious to know.
But, oh, sweet history: I will go down.
And where once I suffered in agony,
now, I shall suffer in peace.

PART V: THE PASSION

1. More of The Collector's Journal, including the eighth poem.

Now Jesus led his people through Galilee and Judea, wending his way to Jerusalem. Once again, from town to town, from the synagogues to the hearthsides to the open fields, he preached to the people. He preached as he had never preached before, speaking new words with a new power. He spoke in parables—and even though few people fully understood what he said, even though his very disciples argued over his meaning, those who heard him seemed to know that he had seen a great thing.

The crowds that came to listen to him grew larger. His fame spread. People said he worked miracles. They said he spoke of the Kingdom of Heaven as if he had been there. They said he was a prophet, in the tradition of John. Those who had been with him beneath the mountain in Perea sometimes said that he was the man who was foretold—the messiah, who would bring the Kingdom to earth himself.

As he neared Jerusalem, it became clear that he intended to enter the city with the Passover; to preach to the Pilgrims even as Rome stood guard. The anticipation all around him increased.

Everywhere he went, there was excitement at his coming.

But Judas, who would betray him finally, came to him and said: "How can you go into the city at Passover? The people will be waiting for any sign of God. The Romans will be

153

waiting for any sign of trouble. Are you going to walk among them, speaking in riddles?"

"Those who have ears to hear with, let them hear," Jesus said.

And he traveled on, telling his tales.

One week before the Passover was to begin, Jesus and his followers came into the suburbs of Jerusalem. They took up lodgings in Bethany, in the house of Simon, whom Jesus had befriended during his days in John's monastery. Here, they waited.

The holiday approached. The pilgrims began to throng the city. The roads leading to Jerusalem's gates became spirals of dust in which could be glimpsed caravans and costumes of every color, from which could be heard the bawling of children, the bray of mules and the psalms of the believers.

And Jesus said: "The time is come."

He led his people to the Mount of Olives, where the prophet Zechariah says the Lord will one day stand. Jesus stood there, amidst the crush of people, and looked down at the city. The moment is chronicled in the collection's penultimate verse:

I have come to you, Jerusalem.
The sun is golden on your walls, the sun like fire.
I have come to speak the name of the Lord
in the place where they call the lamb.

And he joined the crowd—the pilgrims singing and waving their palm leaves in celebration. He walked into the city in the midst of it, and the disciples grew so excited with anticipation

154

they were glancing at the sky, thinking that the Kingdom might suddenly descend.

They entered the city. There was the temple, rearing majestic on the eastern hill. Jesus pushed to the foot of the hill with the mob. With them, he climbed the stairs to the temple wall. They filed through the gate and, as they did, the disciples glanced up at the tower of the Antonia fortress, where the Roman soldiers scanned the crowd, their helmets gleaming.

Jesus, surrounded by his followers, was now in the great outer courtyard. Slowly, he turned his head, surveying the scene. The bright awnings of the merchants were everywhere, flapping lazily in the breeze. The moneychangers were trading shekels for foreign coins so that travelers from distant countries could make their purchases. The pilgrims were haggling over the prices of the animals. The sacrificial lambs were bleating. Jesus' gaze passed over all of them, came to rest, finally, on the solemn colonnade of the temple proper. He smiled.

Then, without speaking, Jesus walked up to the stall of a moneychanger. He placed his hand beneath the coin tray and, in a single sudden motion, flipped it over. The man cried out in protest. His coins spilled across the courtyard, spinning on the pavement, glittering in the sun. Jesus reached up and tore the man's awning from its poles. Its red and white stripes fluttered down around them.

And Jesus shouted like the prophet Jeremiah: "You have turned this house of prayer into a den of thieves!"

The disciples looked on dumbfounded as their leader moved to the next stall, where sacrificial doves were sold. This, too, Jesus destroyed, sending the birds shivering free into the high clouds.

Screaming curses, the temple merchants tried to grab hold of Jesus. But now, the prophet had a knotted cord in his hand and he beat them back. The crowd surged forward to see what was happening. And Jesus turned on them.

At this time, the temple was being rebuilt. Huge stones lay here and there, as did ropes and pulleys. Jesus stepped up onto one of these stones, pointing at it with one hand, pointing out at the upturned faces with the other.

And he shouted out to them in the words of the psalm: " 'The stone that the builder has thrown away has now become the cornerstone!' "

And then he said: "I am Jesus of Nazareth, and I have come to tear this temple down."

Slowly, the courtyard grew still. The people had heard of Jesus, and they had heard he was coming. They gathered around him now to hear what he had to say.

But even before he had begun to speak, the alarm went out to Antonia Tower from the guards below. The legionnaires came thundering across the bridge into the courtyard. Their spears upraised, they headed toward the source of the disturbance.

The people broke from before the soldiers' wedge. The path to Jesus lay clear in front of the oncoming force. But then, Simon shouted out at the top of his voice: "Let him speak! Let the prophet speak!"

The other disciples quickly took up the chant, "Let him speak! Let the prophet speak!" It spread to the people around them. They linked arms, blocking the soldier's path.

The legionnaires halted. They stood silent, afraid of igniting a riot that would send the city up in flames.

Again, Jesus smiled.

"I will tear down this temple that was made with hands," he said, "and by the feast of the Passover, I will build you another, made without hands. I have brought you the Kingdom of Heaven. I tell you: It has already come. It is within you. Listen to me."

And Jesus began to preach. He preached in the courtyard that day, and the next, and the next. Each time, when he was done, he slipped away protected by the mob, and returned to Bethany where he stayed in secret. So he eluded arrest, and returned to preach another day.

And he said: "The Kingdom of Heaven is within you. Listen. There was a father who had two sons. One day, the younger son said to him: 'Father, let me have my portion of the goods.' So the father divided up his living, and gave the boy his portion. The boy left home. He traveled to a distant country. He lived wild, spending his money on whores and drink. Soon enough, he was broke, and hungry. A famine had struck the land, and times were hard. The young man took a job as a hired hand. He went out into his boss' fields to feed the pigs, and he was so hungry, he was ready to eat the corn husks he was throwing to the animals. Finally, he thought to himself: 'This is stupid. My father's servants eat better than this. I'll go home and ask my father's forgiveness. I'll ask him to hire me as a servant, because I've shown myself unworthy to be his son.' So he headed home. Now, when his father saw him coming down the road, he ran out to him at once. He threw his arms around the boy's neck and kissed him. He called to his servants, he said, 'My son! My son is coming home! Bring out the best robe and put it on him! Put a ring on his finger, and shoes on his feet! Bring out the fatted calf and kill it! We'll have a celebration.' Later, the older son came in from the fields where he was working. He heard the sound of the party going on and he asked a servant what it was. When the servant told him, he was furious. He wouldn't go in. His father came out and pleaded with him to enter. But the older son said, 'I've worked and worked for you, Father, all these years, and I've always obeyed you. Not once—not once—have you ever given me a kid so I could celebrate with my friends. My younger brother has wasted his money on whores, and he comes home starving, and for him, you've killed the fatted calf.' And his father answered, 'My son, you were always with me, and all that I have is yours. But isn't it right that we should celebrate when your brother comes home? Because he was dead, and now he's alive again; because he was lost, and now he is found.' "

And Jesus said: "The Kingdom of Heaven is within you. It is like the lord who traveled into a faraway land, and left his goods in the hands of his servants. To one he gave five talents of silver, to another he gave two, and to a third he gave one: each according to his ability. Then he went off. Now, while he was gone, the servant with five talents traded and invested them. Thus, he made another five talents with the first. The one who had two did the same, and he made two more. But the servant who had received only one talent, he thought to himself, 'My master is a hard man, who reaps where he has not sown. Just so I don't lose it, I will bury my talent in the ground.' And so he did. After a long time, then, the master came back and he called his servants to account. The first servant came to him, and said, 'Here are the five talents you left me, and I've made five more.' And the master answered, 'Well done. For this, I will make you a ruler over many things. Enter into the joy of your lord.' The second servant came to him and said, 'Here are the two talents you left me, and with them I made two more.'

And again the master said, 'Well done. For this, I will make
you a ruler over many things. Enter into the joy of your lord.'
And then the third servant came to him and said, 'Master, I
knew you were a hard man, that you reap what you have not
sown, and I was afraid. So that I wouldn't lose it, I have buried
your talent in the ground. Here, take what is yours.' But the
master was furious. He said, 'You lazy idiot. You knew I was a
hard man. Even if you had left the money with the exchangers,
I'd have earned interest on it.' And he called to his guards,
'Take the talent from him and give it to the man with ten. For
to him who has it will be given. From him who has not, even
what he has will be taken away.'"

And Jesus said: "He who has ears to hear with, let him
hear."

And he said: "The Kingdom of Heaven is within you. It's
like the man who went out early in the morning to hire
laborers to work in his vineyard, and they agreed to work for a
penny a day. About the third hour of the day, he saw some men
standing idle in the marketplace, and he said to them, 'Why
don't you go out into the vineyard, too, and I'll pay you
whatever is right.' So they did. About the ninth hour, he hired
some more workers on the same terms, and about the eleventh
hour, he did the same. When evening came, the man said to
his steward, 'Call in the laborers and give them their pay.' And
the men came in—first those who had been hired in the
eleventh hour, then those who had been hired in the ninth and
so on until the first to be hired came in from the fields. And
every man received a penny. Well, the men who were hired first
thought it was unfair. They murmured against the man of the
house. They said they should have been paid more. But the
man answered them, 'My friends, have I done you wrong? You

agreed to work with me for a penny, and you have your penny. As for the rest, it's perfectly legal for me to do what I wish with my own money. Take what's yours and go your way.' "

And Jesus said: "A sower went out into the fields one day and threw his seeds everywhere. Some fell by the wayside and the birds ate them. Some fell on the stony places, and sprung up at once because there was no depth to the earth, and the sun scorched them and because they had no root, they withered away. Some of the seeds fell among thorns and the thorns choked them. And some happened to fall on good ground and brought forth fruit: some thirtyfold, some sixtyfold, some a hundredfold. He who has ears to hear with, let him hear."

The Romans watched him closely. They weren't quite sure what he was saying, but they saw that the people were moved by it, and they considered it dangerous. They enlisted the aid of their allies, the temple priests, the Sadducees, who were only too pleased to challenge the prophet's affront to their authority. The priests sent their agents into the crowd to trick Jesus into heresy or treason, so that the people would desert him and leave him open to arrest.

The agents shouted at him: "John told us to love our neighbor. Who is our neighbor?" And they pointed at Antonia.

And Jesus said: "A man traveling from Jerusalem to Jericho was attacked by thieves. They robbed him and beat him and left him by the road half dead. While the man lay there, a priest came by—and the priest crossed the road to avoid him. Next, a man of the holy family of Levites came by—and he also crossed the road. But a Samaritan—even one of the race whom you despise—happened to be passing. And when he saw the wounded man, he had compassion for him. He went to him, bandaged his wounds. He set him on his mule and brought him to an inn and nursed him there. Even when he left, he said to the innkeeper, 'Take care of this man, and whatever you spend on him, I will repay.' Which of the three—the priest, the Levite or the Samaritan—is the man's neighbor?"

And the agents said: "Should we pay taxes to Rome?"

And Jesus said: "Absolutely. Give them every penny you have. The pennies were made in Caesar's image. You were made in God's. Give Caesar what is Caesar's. Give God what is God's."

Now the Sadducees, impatient with their servants, came forward themselves to tangle Jesus in the obscurest scriptures. And they argued with him in the courtyard once again as they had another time long ago. The Sadducees said: "Moses tells us that the brother of a childless widow should marry her. And if she marries, then, seven times, with whom will she be united come the resurrection of the dead."

And Jesus cried out to them in a transport: "The resurrection of the dead! Isn't it written: 'I am the God of Abraham, and of Isaac and of Jacob'? Don't you see? God is the God of the living, not of the dead. The Kingdom of Heaven is the resurrection of the body. No one is married there or given in marriage. Each is as free as the angels in heaven. This is the body eternal, which does not die! This is the body of children. Come to me like that, come to me like little children. Of such is the Kingdom of Heaven made."

And Jesus said, laughing: "Oh, I will tear this temple down. Tear down this temple that was made with hands and by the Passover I will build you another that was made without hands. I have brought you the Kingdom of Heaven. It is come. Listen to me."

They listened to him. They listened, and they waited. The people waited for the Passover, which they thought would bring the coming of the Kingdom. The Romans and the Sadducees waited for a chance to arrest Jesus away from the crowds.

2. The Book of Judas continued.

And Jesus declared he would travel to Jerusalem, and preach in the temple at Passover. And Judas was amazed, and he said: "Surely, he will cause a disturbance and be arrested." But he saw Jesus had entered the Kingdom of Heaven, and he followed him, waiting to see what would happen.

And Jesus traveled through the countryside, preaching to the people. And he oftentimes spoke now in parables. And Judas tried to comprehend these sayings, but his thoughts were too much on Mary; for she had turned away from him, believing they had sinned when they lay together.

Now, one day, Judas saw Mary listening to Jesus preach. And her eyes were filled with tears. And when she hurried away, Judas followed her and found her kneeling by a river and crying.

And Judas approached her, saying: "Why are you crying, my beloved?"

And Mary said: "I'm afraid of myself, and God."

And Judas could not restrain himself and said: "Oh, my love, why have you abandoned me?"

And she answered, saying: "Judas, haven't we sinned a great sin, because we lay together?"

And Judas cried out to her:

"It is no sin, no sin to be a human being.
It is no sin to be a creature of the flesh."

And taking hold of his own breast he said: "I love you."

And Mary said: "Don't come near me anymore. I am consecrated to the Kingdom."

And she turned and ran away from him.

And when Jesus reached Jerusalem, he began straightway to preach in the temple. And his sayings and deeds caused a great agitation among the people. And Judas saw that the temple priests were enraged; they conspired with the Romans to arrange the preacher's arrest. But during the day, they feared the people, and at night, Jesus escaped them and retired to a house in Bethany.

And the people flocked to hear Jesus. And they spoke among themselves, saying, "Perhaps this is he who has been foretold. We will await the coming of the Kingdom at Passover."

And Judas heard these sayings, and feared an uprising. And one evening, when Jesus was walking alone in the courtyard in Bethany, Judas approached him, saying: "Rabbi."

And Jesus said: "Yes."

And Judas asked him: "Why do you speak in riddles to the people? I have seen them turning their eyes to the sky, waiting for the Kingdom to come down."

And Jesus laughed and said: "Those who have ears to hear with, let them hear."

And Judas said: "But they are stirred up with expectations. They will rise up against the Romans in great numbers, and in great numbers they will be killed."

And Jesus answered him gently, saying: "Judas, my friend, you are fighting an old fight over and over."

And Judas grew angry in his heart and shouted: "And you

are keeping an old engagement with death, and will drag my people with you."

And Jesus said: "Judas, Judas, look to yourself. Even the Kingdom of Hell is in the Kingdom of Heaven."

And Judas said: "I will look to my people. I would rather the soldiers arrest you here in secret than in the city where it might cause a bloodbath."

And Judas covered his mouth, ashamed by what he had said.

But Jesus said to him: "Do what you have to do."

And Judas cried out in his confusion, saying: "Rabbi, Rabbi, help me. Say the thing that will help me."

And Jesus lay his hand upon Judas' shoulder, and said, "Remember Lot's wife."

And Jesus left Judas alone in the courtyard. And Judas sank down upon the earth on his knees. And covering his eyes, he cried out to the Lord for guidance. But the Lord was silent to him.

And after a time had passed, Judas arose from the ground. And he said in anguish:

"I who have seen the heart of love in ashes,
I who have seen the heart of fear in arms:
I must make a voice for myself in the ears of my people.
I am called to the battlefield one more time."

And he began to plan Jesus' secret arrest to prevent a slaughter in the temple.

165

3. More of the Tale of Mary Magdalene.

Now Jesus has come to Jerusalem to preach on the Passover. He stays in a house in Bethany. There, Mary is making the unleavened bread. And she thinks: "I only wanted. But I only wanted. Could I tell her, ask her, Sarah, beside me: What should I do? Oh, she's thinking: I wish my mother were here, I would ask her. She is so worried for them, looks more like Susannah every day, her high brow wrinkling with worry for them. Oh, I wish I had died. I told him, I said, 'I wish I had died before I lay with you again.' It hurt him. 'Don't say that,' he said. And I said it again because I wanted to hurt him, him so big and me just seventeen. I said it again. But it wasn't true. I know. I know. It's just, he doesn't understand, it's just when he came down, when Jesus came down from the mountain, and I saw him, and I saw his black eyes running deep into the tunnel of everything and then beyond and he was smiling and I fell on my knees on the stony ground, the sharp rocks digging into the joints and Judas still dripping warm down my thighs, well I did wish . . . I don't know. I don't know what to do. Should I ask her, she's already 'Is anything wrong, Mary?' trying to replace Susannah but I don't know I don't know. When Judas—we were in the orchard yesterday, and the cool steady breeze came down the rows and blew my hair across my face as I turned away and he caught my arm in his big hand and when he said, 'I saw what happened, Mary, when I was in you. Everything was all right then, wasn't it? Wasn't it?' I

shook my head, the tears starting behind the strands of hair
blowing over my eyes because I was just—confused. Because it
did seem all right then when he was in me and I wanted to kiss
and kiss him I did as he filled and filled me and it was like
there was nothing but that nothing but that and everything
lacing branches pinioned in their barkgray by the sudden
rising of the sun and I couldn't believe how how how *simple* it
was, everything, no way to say it but just but just the trees,
sun, sky, and the big white moon not sinking earth between
my buttocks cock in and out of my cunt lips on my lips forever
ending I don't know. But then, when he came down. From the
mountain. That's why I said it. In the orchard, when he said,
'Everything was all right then, wasn't it? Wasn't it?' Shook my
head, the taste of my hair on my lips, salty, said, 'It wasn't. It
wasn't. I wish I had died first.' And he said, 'Don't say that.'
'It's true,' I said. 'I wish I had died before I lay with you again.'
And it hurt him and he ran his hand up trembling through his
hair the way he does when he's filled with something and he
can't say it, and it always makes me want to hold him, and he
said, 'All right, all right, it doesn't matter now. It doesn't
matter. We have to get away, that's all. You have to get away.
You don't know what he's doing in the city. They don't
understand him. They think something is going to happen at
the Passover, they don't . . .' And I was so confused because
when he came down, Jesus, from the mountain, with his eyes
all filled with the godlight and I was so afraid afraid I fell to
my knees of him swallowing me back into the darkness of his.
I shouted, 'Why couldn't you have just taken me away then?
Why did you bring me here in the first place?' And Judas said,
'Listen to me, Mary, please. There's going to be an uprising.
You can hear them talking about it everywhere when Jesus is in

the city. They don't understand what he's saying. They don't understand what Rome is. The days of the Maccabees are over.' And when I didn't understand either, when I just looked at him because he wasn't answering what I, he said, 'Pilate's too strong now. He'll slaughter them in the streets. The blood. Oh, Mary, it's so horrible. It's not like they say.' I started to cry. His big roughgentle hand. Smoothed the hair away from my face. 'Come with me,' he said. 'We can make something of it. What we had. We had everything there is.' I said, I was so confused, I said, 'Why didn't you say it before he came down the mountain?' because when he came down the mountain I could see, could see in his eyes that he had found, that it had come to him, everything, everything there is, come to him, really just like in my dream, in the first bright bolt of sunlight over the eastern mountain ranges, only not to pierce him, not to enter him, only to show him—and what it showed him he became. I could see that. See that he was something new, that he didn't just know things anymore, that he was them somehow, and I don't know what to do because there's blood, so much blood, in the earth at hand and little babies they drown in the weeds for no good reason and mommies and daddies can't be better than themselves and they hurt and hurt you and men, they kill each other, and women, they kill themselves I don't know I don't know what I mean it's just all so awful and the sun had risen and he'd become the sweetness of all the world like the juicy morning figs under the striped awning when the breeze comes into the square from the sea and I fell to my knees I wanted to take him into my mouth and suck and suck the goodness of it he'd become and it was all so so impossible because a moment ago I could have would have been Jesus' alone only then he would've swallowed me, de-

voured me because he would have been just like the reflection
in the wading pond and I would have seen him as *I* was now,
and now, I'd had Judas under the branches and I'd seen
something too something of my own and I wanted wanted to
hold on couldn't, couldn't . . . become . . . know . . . what
to do. I asked him. I said, 'Judas, what will you do?' Because
he'd said to me, said to me, 'If you stay, I'll have to stay. I can't
leave you to it. And if I stay, I'll have to try to stop him before
. . . before the killing starts.' And I said to him, 'Judas, what
will you do?' And he said, 'They're asking for him, in the
crowds. Spies the priests send out for the Romans. They're
afraid to arrest him while the people are there and they want to
know where he goes.' 'Judas.' I heard his name, my voice,
floating away up and down the orchard rows. 'Judas.' 'He
doesn't understand,' he said. 'His mystic vision! The city will
go up in flames.' And when I would not answer him, he left
me there in the orchard rows, with my hair matted to my
cheeks not even blowing because the tears had made it heavy
and damp. But how could I? Answer him. He doesn't see how
everything is just so impossible now. Impossible to move, act,
choose. Should I tell? Should I tell Jesus? Should I ask Sarah:
Should I tell? What would happen to Judas then? What would
he say? What—what—what would he say to me? Because I am
so afraid. So. Of dying, of being cut free of Jesus who took me
out of the dying. Of the children dying, of becoming the
women who watch the children die. Of losing him Judas oh I
do wish I had died before I let him touch me it was so much
simpler before I'm so afraid. I look at Sarah, watch her. I see
her high brow wrinkling worried too for Simon she still thinks
hopes they will have children playing leapfrog in the courtyards laughing in the heat which makes even the women do

their duties with slow hands pausing to wipe the sweat from their foreheads with their sleeves while the children jump over each other, tumble in the dust and always laughing because they dream but they don't remember their dreams and they know but don't believe how dire love is, how you look into his eyes and they are tunnels even into the vaults of the things you want most secretly and the darkness of them is a light that pierces you and fills you with your unbearable self and whenever he stands on the hilltops and speaks I feel him travel into me into the place I am so that he lives in what I am and I am only the light of him knowing and then and then I am so afraid afraid and I feel it whispering in me let him be done let him be gone let him be over forever because if I open to him once now he will come into me with the full force of himself and his knowing and I I I I will be nothing nothing nothing.

4. The end of The Collector's Journal, including the ninth, and final, verse in the cycle.

At last, the evening of the feast arrived. Simon and John went into the city and arranged for the group to eat at a guest house. Then they went to the temple and sacrificed the lamb.

When the others arrived for the meal, the women and servants set to preparing the food in the inn downstairs. Above, in the upper room, the men sat at table, with Jesus at the head.

The women brought in cups full of wine and placed them on the table. Jesus raised his cup and said: "Blessed art thou, O Lord, who created the fruit of the vine."

He drank, and the others drank as well.

The women brought in bowls of bitter herbs, and the sauce made of almonds and dates and figs. They placed them on the table.

Jesus raised a portion of the herbs and the sauce.

He said: "Blessed art thou, O Lord, who created the fruits of the earth."

He ate, and the others ate as well.

Jesus poured a second cup of wine. He said: "Our father brought us out of slavery in the land of Egypt with a mighty hand, and we are free. And he slaughtered the sons of the Egyptians. But the angel of death passed over the houses of the Jews. We made the mark of the blood of the lamb upon our doors and the angel of death passed over. Tonight, we eat the lamb of God who died for us, and we remember that we are free."

Jesus drank, and sang the hymn which begins: "Praise the Lord. Praise, oh you servants of the Lord, the name of the Lord. Blessed is the name of the Lord from this time forth and forevermore."

Mary brought the platter of unleavened bread and laid it before him. He broke a piece and dipped it in the sauce. The others followed him.

He said: "Blessed art thou, O Lord, who caused the earth to bring forth bread."

He ate, and the others ate as well.

The women brought in the lamb, and the feast began. Everyone ate and drank heartily.

Finally, it was time for the last drink of wine. Jesus lifted his cup. He smiled and nodded at the disciples. His face was drawn now and his eyes were weary.

He said: "I've been longing and longing to sit down with you all so we could eat this meal together. You are the ones who were with me in Capernaum when it began. John and James . . . Levi . . . All of you. Simon . . ." But his lips began to tremble, his eyes filled with tears. For a moment, he could not continue.

Then he said: "Now, one of you is going to betray me."

The others cried out in dismay. Several of them jumped to their feet. A cup was turned over and the red wine stained the table. Everyone seemed to be shouting: "Tell us who it is, tell us."

But Jesus shook his head. He looked around him. The voices died. Slowly, the disciples realized what their prophet was saying. Those who had risen sank back to their seats. Some covered their faces. Some stared at Jesus with tear-stained cheeks. Some could not look at him at all.

Jesus smiled. He picked up the unleavened bread that lay before him on the table. He broke it and handed a piece to Simon, who sat beside him. He said: "Here. Take this bread, each of you. Eat it. This is my body."

The bread was passed from hand to hand and each of them ate it, even Judas Sicariot, who was the traitor.

Now Jesus lifted the wine cup before him. And he said: "Drink this wine. This is my blood."

The cup was passed around and each of them drank.

No one could speak.

Then, in a loud voice, Jesus began to sing the final hymn, which ends: "God is the Lord, who has showed us light: Bind the sacrifice with cords to the altar horns. Thou art my God, and I will praise thee; thou art my God, I will exalt thee. O give thanks to the Lord, for he is good; for his mercy endures forever."

And then the feast was over.

Jesus stood. He spoke to Simon and James and John, the very first to be with him. He said: "Come with me into the olive grove. I want to pray."

The four went out of the city to the Mount of Olives. The full moon was shining. They went up the hillside to the grove called Gethsemane. When they had entered and walked among the trees a little, Jesus stopped and turned to his three friends. He was sweating, and his voice shook.

He said: "I must be alone. I am sick to death with sadness. Stay here, and let me be alone for a while."

He left them and walked on. Simon and James and John sat down on the ground. They gazed at each other sadly.

175

"There will be trouble for all of us, when it comes," John said.

"We must stand by him," said James.

"We will," said Simon. "Now and forever."

Then, overcome by the food and wine, their heads fell forward, and they were asleep.

Alone, Jesus walked until he came into a clearing. There, he fell to his knees. Trembling violently, he clasped his hands before him. His eyes scanned the garden wildly.

Here, then, is the final verse in the collection:

The moon, and no stars.
The silver silhouettes of olive branches, humped, bending.
The air—the cool air—
the little wind that doesn't even blow.
The fear (I do not want to die), the sadness.
The mother by the well in spring.
nasteeda-nasteeda . . .
sparrow in darkness, singing.
Mighty in birdsong templesinging
preaching in the courtyard
woman by the courtyard wall
blackmelted plungebeckon eyes
breastnibble smile, a half smile
birdsinging pout—oh oh oh—
the sleeping childbed, all ears—
the child all ears.
Flogged will I erect before them
father-forsaken mother-divine
bagod carnivorous incarnate—
(no one spoke the name of the Lord)

176

shewinsome deathfucked
sucking god's cup of death?
This is my body. This is my blood.
Oh, Father, why did you forsake me?
Let this cup pass. Let this cup pass.
Lark lark lark oh miserable
not to remember, not to remember the lark.
This night.
This night of moonlight and no stars.
Flutterdust beams, motherplunge eye of night:
embrace—if I could have told them
to embrace—it is not finished, John!
Storyless grave. Oh well, Jesus, old son,
life is like that. Storyless life.
A stone within the loneness of a lark
sunk thuddingly and soddenly I broke . . .
Who was that woman that I never loved
who, sweet-created in regret,
creates not, neither does she live?
Leaden balls purblind to infanteyed mortality,
clawfists scrabbling at the little wind,
lipdust whispering: embrace! embrace!
So she will find me and mourn me mad
making madness of me,
walling up the resurrection with the dead.
Yet it is finished.
Storyless: She never might have whispered to me.
But who then will not retell my life in silence?
Yes, it is finished.
That still air the moonlight shows
to be invisible; that the trees lift into:

177

Son of Man

The dead are not dead.
Now, she cannot help but whisper me:
I am the way of the living:
Theirs is the moment mine.
The moonmoment and no stories and no stars;
the little wind that does not even blow;
the nightwork of branches in silver solitude:
Yes, it is finished; all, all, all!
Even the dreams of kisses, even the face I loved,
even the map of tears, the shadow,
the shit, the wine, the earth like honey . . .
Ah. Look at it. Look at it.
I could go on forever!

5. The conclusion of the Book of Judas.

Now when the feast of the Passover had come, Jesus and his disciples gathered at a guest house in Jerusalem. And Jesus was weary and trembling. And he said to them: "I am glad to eat this feast with you who have been with me through all my temptations. For soon now, one of you is going to betray me."

And Judas was among them, for he still was undecided what to do. And when he heard these words, his heart was like a stone, and he wondered if Jesus would name him.

But instead, Jesus quieted the outcry of his disciples. And he broke the unleavened bread, and passed it among them. And he said to them: "Take this. Eat it. This is my body."

And the disciples ate the bread. And when Judas ate, it tasted like meat upon his tongue.

And Jesus passed the wine among them and said to them: "Take this. Drink it. This is my blood."

And the disciples drank the wine. And when Judas drank, the wine was thick and warm.

And when the meal was finished, Jesus rose and said: "I will go out to the grove of Gethsemane to pray." And aside, he said to Judas: "What you must do, do quickly." For he did not want the soldiers to find his disciples with him.

And when Jesus was gone, Judas rose from his place, and went down the ladder to the ground. And he passed the door of the house and saw Mary inside, cleaning the plates. And his mouth was filled with the taste of the bread and wine, and he

179

could not speak to her. And his eyes were wild as if he would go mad.

And Judas ran along the alleys of the night. And he ran to the house of Caiaphas, who was the chief priest. And Caiaphas was sitting in the great hall of his house, surrounded by many men of importance. And they were eating rich dishes from plates of silver, and drinking fine wines from goblets encrusted with jewels. And Caiaphas performed the ceremonies, setting out a chalice of wine for the coming of Elijah. But Judas came in, bursting past the servants at the gate.

And Judas said: "The man from Nazareth is in the garden of Gethsemane. You can arrest him there in secret."

And Caiaphas dabbed his mouth with a cloth. And he said to his servants: "Give this man some money." For he had sent agents among the people to offer a reward to those who would disclose Jesus' whereabouts. But Judas turned and left the house, taking no money with him.

Now, Judas ran to the Mount of Olives and entered the grove of Gethsemane. And he found Jesus standing in a clearing with Simon and James and John. And Judas embraced Jesus and kissed him on the cheek.

And he said: "I hardly know what I have done."

And Jesus said: "God help you."

Now at that moment, they heard the cries of a mob. And it was the servants of the high priest armed with swords and clubs.

And Simon and James and John were afraid. And Jesus said to them: "Go." And John and James ran from the grove as quickly as they could. But Simon stood still. And he drew from his belt a small sword like the one Judas carried, and he displayed it to Jesus.

And he said: "I will never abandon you."

And Jesus heard the priest's servants at the entrance of the grove. And he pushed Simon's sword away gently. And he smiled, saying: "If you live by the sword, my friend, you'll die by it."

And Simon knew that he must leave.

And he said: "I will . . . I will . . ."

But he could not finish. And he turned and ran from the grove.

And the mob burst in and surrounded Jesus and Judas.

But Caiaphas was with them and he pointed at Judas, saying: "Set this man free. He is one of us."

Then word spread of the prophet's capture. And the rebels called for an uprising in the city. But the people would not join them. And the Romans arrested the rebel leaders, and the riot was done.

And the chief priests consulted with the elders and scribes. And they bound Jesus with ropes and carried him away to be tried by Pilate for civil crimes. For they hated the man, for he had challenged them in the temple, and they wanted him put to death.

And Pilate waited until the days of the feast were over before calling the case; and he released the rebels to their families to demonstrate his leniency, because he wanted no more trouble among the people. And the people condemned Jesus to each other, because he had promised them the Kingdom, but he had no power against Rome.

And Jesus was brought before Pilate. And the priests spoke against him and accused him of treason, saying: "He exhorted the people to tear down the temple. And he claimed he would establish a new kingdom over Rome."

And Pilate questioned Jesus, saying: "Are you, then, the king of the Jews?" And Jesus was silent, so that Pilate shouted at him: "Speak!" But Jesus said nothing.

And Pilate raised his hand angrily, saying: "I sentence you to die on the cross. Bailiff, tie him up, and have him flogged."

And Jesus was dragged into a courtyard and tied to a pole. And a soldier whipped him until his back was covered with blood. Then he was thrown into a dungeon with others who had been condemned.

And in the morning, Jesus was brought into the yard with a number of those criminals. And they were given nothing but rags to cover their loins. And the soldiers herded them through the streets of the city to a hill called Golgotha. And there, they nailed them all to wooden crosses by their hands. And they tied their hands, and set their legs astride wooden pegs. And then the soldiers lifted the crosses into the air. And the moans of the victims were loud among them.

And people gathered to watch the execution, and they jeered at Jesus as he died, saying: "Oh, you there, who was going to tear down the temple and build it again in three days, why don't you try climbing down from the cross?" And even the criminals who died with him taunted him.

But Jesus went to the cross in silence. And he cried out when his hands were nailed, and again when they lifted the cross, but then he said no more. And after he had been on the cross three days, he let out a last cry, and he was dead.

And during this time, the disciples did not come to Golgotha, because they feared being recognized by the crowd and arrested. But the women were there: Mary Magdalene, and Sarah, and other women who had come down with him into Jerusalem.

And when all the crucified were dead, the soldiers took them down from their crosses. And they dumped Jesus' body and all the others into a shallow pit, and covered them over with earth.

Now, when Judas was told that his friend was dead, he wandered through the city drunken, and weeping.

And he returned to Gethsemane at night and sat alone there in the darkness beneath the stars. And he removed from his cloak the small sword which he kept with him. And he said: "My name is murder."

And he fell upon the weapon, and died.

6. The conclusion of the Tale of Mary Magdalene.

Mary thinks: "It is finished. Finally. I thought we would never be done. The lamb alone took hours on the open flame. And keeping them in bread and sauces and wine I must have been up those stairs a hundred times. It was sad to see them, gathered around talking for the last time; to think: I'll never have the chance to feed them again and have them look up from their conversation to smile at me. But it is finished now. And at least . . . At least he knows. At least, at least there was nothing for me to do there, nothing to decide, no one to choose. I don't know what I would have done, I was all on edge and waiting for the proper moment and not knowing really what I would do when the moment came and my thoughts going this way and that faster and faster and then, then he said to them, I could hear him as I came downstairs, said, 'One of you is going to turn me over to the authorities soon.' And I heard all the cries and then the conversation blurring behind me as I came down the stairs, as I stood by the wine board, one hand on the big amphora, gazing away where Sarah and Deborah and the others blurred in front of me it was like a dream. He knew. They'd had it out the two of them. I knew they would. And for it seemed a long time I could only think that it was sad that all of them would never be together talking again, leaning toward each other, with everything so important and profound and me bringing them the wine and the food and them pausing even from the brink of a thought to

185

turn to smile to thank me not a whore anymore. For a long time, that was all I could think about and that it was finished, it was all right. He knew. Of course he would. Of course. And then I thought about him dying, I saw him dying. In the foggy, dreamy gaze as I stood there, I saw him taken away to die, tangled in the seaweed arms of the soldiers and the rabbis dragging him down down down down. And then, suddenly clear out of the blurry murmuring upstairs, suddenly the way the moon is when a thin haze of clouds you barely knew was there passes away from it and every detail of it is clear in the sky, I heard him say, 'Take this, eat this, this is my body.' And my hand went out, unseeing, to the board before me until my fingertips were grainy with the broken fragments of un-leavened bread. And I brought my fingers to my lips and tasted it and it was warm and soft and full of substance and then dissolving, his body, and his body was all there was of him to have because as I tasted it I was not gazing blindly anymore but seeing Sarah pass behind the ceiling post an empty platter in her hands pass before the open door her figure framed in night and the silver darkness of the moon and in the moment and he said, 'Take this and drink it. This is my blood,' and I felt my right hand on the rugged glaze of clay—the neck of the amphora—and my left encompassing the little bowl and moving it beneath the jug tilting easily on its fulcrum and how I saw the red wine pour, the splash and sparkle of it in the candlelight the light stretched over the flow of it, moving with the flow of it but never gone from the flow of it into the cup and I set the amphora right and lifted the cup to my lips and drank his blood, his life, his life and death, the life and death of his body which was in me and all there was and never ending never not dying never not living one thing being the one thing forever. And then I shivered. Someone walking on my grave, I guess. An odd thought: your grave being out there somewhere for someone to walk on. I shivered, and it was finished, all of it. Finished and done like I had come to the brink of something and then pulled away even before. Even before I knew. I was there. I was calm. I'm still calm, still standing here just scared and full of sadness. Sadness for the old things that are going away. This is my body. The Kingdom is the resurrection of the body. If you could fall like that. If you could fall into the mourning oh it would be like a kind of swimming like you fell into the pond and fought and fought against going under and then finally gave in and found you were a mermaid really and could swim beneath the ripples empty of everything but the sun forever I don't know. That sadness. That sadness, though. There is so much dying to get done. That's the story. You have to listen to the story like a child, Judas. Judas, if we'd known. Lips softer than caresses soft as lips. Jesus has gone out to Gethsemane now. I wonder if they'll come for him there, tonight. They will come for him. They will take him. I hope they do it quickly, not like John. Lay him in the caves. Let it be over. Let it be over and done. Later, I will go out there to the tomb. This is my body. I will go out I will go out and what was that out there I thought. I thought. Brr. The nerves. Waiting for them. I'd better pull myself together, anyhow. I have to help Sarah with the clearing away."

THE END